Just Desserts

I0593612

NJ Gallegos

BLACK HARE PRESS SHORT READS

FINGERPRINT FORENSICS SHORT READS

DEAD MAN WALKING by DAVID GREEN

MR HANGMAN by SCOTT MCGREGOR

HELL HARE HOUSE SHORT READS

SEEING by PATRICK WINTERS

RAINMAKER by BILL HUGHES

TESATO'S CODE by KAREN BAYLY

THE PUB AT CROKERS CROSSING by KRIS ASHTON

THE DEVIL AND THE LOCH ARD GORGE by LEANBH PEARSON

SANCTUARY by MICHAEL J. STIEHL

JUST DESSERTS by NJ GALLEGOS

SOMETHING IN MY EYE by TERRI HAMILL

CLOWN DIARY – APPENDIX 7 by JOE OPPENHEIMER

Edited by Jodi Christensen
Formatting by Ben Thomas
Cover design by Dawn Burdett

Connect: linktr.ee/blackharepress

Dedicated to my supportive wife who always encourages me to follow my dreams

and to my high school arch nemesis...you know who you are.

Contents

Chapter One

S ue parsed through the offerings the postman left in the mailbox. Every day (excluding holidays, which bizarrely still included Columbus Day even though America cried out each year over the explorer's complete dickhead status) the mail truck trustily trundled down the street, no matter the snow, the rain, the heat. They never seemed to be out during the "gloom of night" like their motto said, but she could forgive them that. Neither was she.

She flicked the red mailbox door shut, which latched with a metallic *clang!* Her jaw clenched at the noise, at the reminder. Every damn day (excluding those handy federal holidays) she suffered embarrassment when she retrieved the mail.

When she was still in elementary school, her mother paid a local woodworker to build a specialty mailbox, emblazoned with bright yellow lettering that was supposed to resemble drippy mustard spelling out their last name: Moore. The mustardy Moore was prominently displayed on either side of a red wooden hot dog nestled into a brown bun; the whole monstrosity mounted on a stake implanted in the ground. Green grass in the summer, brown dregs during all the other seasons.

Even worse?

It wasn't your standard Oscar Mayer hot dog. The front of the box was designed to look like a

12

Dachshund with a toothy grin and bulbous eyes that gazed in opposite directions.

"He has blew eyes! Blew eyes? Yeah, the wind blew one that way and the other that way!"

Add the damn mailbox to the long list of subjects she was endlessly bullied about in school. *"Hey Susie! Maybe your stupid mailbox can be your date to the prom. It's not like anyone else is gonna ask you! You might get lucky and you can sit on its face and get a splinter in your twat!"*

Frankly, she found it surprising that some testosterone fueled jock with a small dick complex hadn't taken a baseball bat to the poor dog.

The sun beat down on her face, the spring heat teasing at the scorching summer weather to come. Perfect for weenie roasts and sweating bottles of beer in the backyard. Idle conversations about nothing in particular. Maybe a nice game of cornhole or horseshoes. Her eyes narrowed, sensitive to the brightness overwhelming the day.

Damn. She should have grabbed the floppy hat she normally wore when she was busy in the yard, plucking stubborn weeds from the garden or trimming the Oleander shrubs whose arms were constantly threatening to spill out on the sidewalk. She pressed her right hand against her forehead, making a poor man's visor, bathing her eyes in blessed shadow. With her other hand, she shuffled through her mail haul with the efficiency of a card shark cutting a new hand.

A glossy new issue of Redbook (an aging actress smiled up at her, her forehead lineless and expressionless, promising to reveal *Her Secret For Successful Marriage*; a relevant topic for an actress on her fifth marriage), her mother was sure to be thrilled; a bill from her recent doctor's visit (her Prozac dosage dialed up again, what with the daily passive thoughts of jerking her car's steering wheel into oncoming traffic); another bill, this one from her therapist (but how does that make you feel, Sue?); and—

—a plain white envelope addressed to her with no return address.

Who would send her mail?

Her brow furrowed in concentration as she raised the envelope up to the sun, hoping for a hint of the contents inside. She didn't have any friends... unless you counted the geriatric woman that worked the front desk at the library she frequented at least once a week. They shared a fondness for guilty pleasure bodice ripping romances.

Definitely not a birthday invite. The thought of even being invited to a party made her involuntarily chuckle. She remembered kids handing out birthday invites in class and they'd always detoured around her as if repelled by a secret force field. One only the cool kids could feel.

Less likely a ransom request, maybe some good ol' fashioned anthrax spores? Nah, probably not, but it would be an interesting turn of events, that's for sure.

Using her index finger, she ripped open the envelope and was rewarded with a fresh bloom of pain that shot up her digit. Beads of blood welled up from a thin paper cut. *Jesus!* Frowning, she plopped the wounded digit in her mouth, tasting copper and considered her mail.

"It's Time For…" read the front. On either side of the bold lettering stood a tiger sporting a mischievous looking grin. He wore an orange letterman jacket that clung to his bulging shoulder muscles and had his elbow propped up on the letters.

That tiger—

Her feet suddenly felt as if they were encased in cement blocks. She was rooted to the ground, and a lightning bolt might as well have descended from the sky, enveloping her in its fury. Her heart began a frantic tap dance against her ribs.

Tap, tap, tap.

Each tap increased the ever-so-charming tightening sensation in her throat, just like that time in high school that she—

No, not the time to bring *that* mess up.

It was Tom the Tiger, the grinning, handsome (if you were into animals) mascot of her high school. It seemed he was still hounding her all these years later.

His green eyes bored into her own and damned if she didn't see a twinkle dance through their black pupils, paper tiger or not. His dark eyebrows were arched in an expression of supreme humor, as if he were saying, *"Hey there Sue, you fuckin' nerd, you remember me, right?"*

Sweat dotted her palms, sticking the back of

the card to her skin, and her hands shook while pins and needles invaded her fingertips. The rest of the mail tumbled down to the cracked, raised sidewalk. Thick muscles in her jaw contracted, painfully clamping her mouth shut. Faint squeaking noises emitted from her, sounding like the bouncing mattress springs in a honeymoon suite at a budget hotel. Each night she popped in a mouthguard to prevent the horrid gnashing of her teeth. Luckily her headgear had gone the way of the dodo. Sharp daggers stole into her temples, setting up shop, promising a corker of a migraine later. Her mouth twisted into a rictus of repulsion that stuttered here and there with the grinding of her teeth. She was certain that she looked insane and any neighbor that spied her in this state might decide that a 911 call was in order.

Anthrax would have been a better present, hands down.

Just Desserts

Slow … deep … breath … in through the nose, out through the mouth.

Responding to the words, to the oft-repeated mantra, her heart slowed, and the numbness melted away in her fingertips.

She was regaining control.

It wouldn't do to have a crying fit in the front yard. That's how rumors about the crazy neighbors gained their footholds. *Hey did you hear? That weird girl from next door opened an envelope and went batshit, total cuckoo bananas. I heard she eats cat food and yowls at the moon too!* She considered what size of straitjacket she might need and then admonished herself. *Stop being a wuss and open the damn card.*

The inside of the card showed a furry tiger paw clutching a bunch of floating orange and black balloons by their strings.

Printed in massive block letters:

"Our 20-Year High School Reunion!"

In print underneath:

"Can you believe it? It's been twenty years already! More details to come. Please join the AHS Class of 2001 Facebook group to learn more!"

It was signed by Lauren Georgia-Smith, Class of 2001, Class President. It was a flowery signature, reeking of contempt. A lopsided heart dotted the 'i' in Smith.

Sue's breakfast of dry toast and coffee frantically pushed the large red button marked "evacuate" and rose to the back of her throat, threatening to make a spectacular reappearance. Her stomach flip-flopped, doing its best Olympic gymnast impression, hoping for straight tens across the board. *Gulp!* She swallowed hard and winced as her esophagus spasmed with the effort of returning the (probably) tan colored puke back to its rightful place.

Just Desserts

Lauren Georgia...now Georgia-Smith—someone must have married the bitch. Perhaps Satan, but then her last name would be Georgia-Lucifer or maybe Georgia-Beelzebub.

And even Satan had his standards.

Ugh, Lauren Georgia with her stupid little upturned nose, full lips with perfectly applied cherry lip gloss, bleach blonde hair that lightened to nearly white in the summer, thanks to her lifeguarding job. She flounced about with her tight, gorgeous body in a cheerleader uniform, always hanging around the jocks. Reveling at how their eyes bulged out of their heads in pleasure at the sight of her. Her tongue was pure acid, spitting venom whenever Sue was unlucky enough to come within striking distance. Most regarded the inland taipan as the most venomous snake in the world, but Sue could point some confused zoologists in the right direction.

Straight towards Lauren Georgia; now Lauren Georgia-Smith.

That cunt never missed an opportunity to humiliate Sue, especially if she had an audience. Attention seeking bitch. Word on the street was that her daddy up and left the family. Went for a pack of smokes and made like an egg and beat it. Maybe *that* was what fucked her up. But that was making excuses for her behavior. Sue suspected that the truth was simpler than that.

The bitch was rotten to the core.

Her preferred stage was the locker room, before P.E. class commenced. The stale sweat smell and grody puke green lockers certainly added to the ambiance. Sue gravitated to a dark corner where the bulb had burned out last spring, taking refuge in the shadows. Unfortunately, Lauren had a nose for Sue's whereabouts, might have even implanted a microchip to track her every move.

Just Desserts

Sue folded herself into the gloomy corner, changing with the hustle of an actor backstage of a live production preparing for the next scene. Her speed ultimately meant nothing. Lauren would saunter by, her perky boobs enclosed in a trendy bright pink Victoria's Secret bra, and she would pretend to trip, colliding theatrically with Sue. Bonus points were awarded if she caused Sue's head to thump woodenly on her open locker door. Other times she would "spill" a bottle of sticky sweet tea, shuffling her feet in a mockery of stumbling with Oscar-worthy precision, soaking both the floor and Sue. Her aim was true and usually she coated both Sue's gym clothes and street clothes with the sugary concoction. The rest of the day would be spent in swampy, sticky clothes that attracted bees each time she went outside. A charming side effect. At least she wasn't allergic to *them.*

"Whoops! I'm s-s-s-s-o-o s-s-s-s-s-o-o-w-w-w-y!" She would sing-song, pitching her voice high, careful to mimic Sue's stutter and speech impediment down to the letter. She would toss her blonde mane back and strut off, sometimes taking a bow as the other wannabe bitches clapped and cackled.

Sue's face grew painfully hot at the memory, shamed still even twenty years later.

"Fat chance I'm going to that reunion," she muttered to herself. *Riiiiiipppp*, she twisted the card, tearing it into small pieces as she walked inside, tossing the remains in the trash can.

She'd missed her ten year reunion, not that she planned on attending, but the psychiatric hospital surely wouldn't have granted her a day pass for the event. Not even if she asked, "pretty please with a cherry on top?".

She plopped down on the kitchen chair,

tapping her fingers and jiggling her legs to a beat only she could hear called "the anxiety shuffle". *Maybe I should take a Xanax.*

The orange prescription bottle sat on the counter, right next to her laptop, and she grabbed both and sat back down. She shook the bottle into her palm, one nice blue pill, then reconsidered, shaking out two and dry swallowed them.

Better.

Time to surf the web. Maybe she could find some Xena fan fiction she hadn't read yet. Luckily there were plenty of fellow nerds out in the world that hungered to know more about Xena's and Gabrielle's "friendship" and they had no problem penning steamy stories that shipped the couple. She turned on her laptop, watched as it powered up with some scattered groans from deep within the circuitry, and her Doctor Who background filled the screen. While she waited, she ran a finger along the sliver-thin raised scar on her throat.

She opened the browser, planning to type in the link that took her to her favorite fanfic site, but she helplessly watched her fingers tap in Facebook's address instead. Her damned hands acted like they had brains of their own!

She'd never had a Facebook account and was prompted to create one, listing her date of birth, hometown, high school and the like. She left the profile picture blank. Suggestions popped up, friends she might know based on her profile information and damned if that bitch wasn't front and center—Lauren Georgia-Smith. The twat was smiling at the camera surrounded by picture perfect clones, one boy and one girl, while a handsome brunette man—her husband then—stood behind her. The man's hands were wrapped around Lauren's waist, laying claim on his prize. Bleh.

"Close the laptop, go read a book, jump off a

cliff, anything but this," a voice whispered to her.
She considered heeding its advice, but her traitorous
finger clicked down on the profile picture.

More pictures of the wonderful happy family;
a nauseating Christmas Card picture where they all
wore matching ugly sweaters (the family golden
retriever also sported a matching sweater, a goofy
grin plastered on his face); a list of groups Lauren
belonged to (chief among them was the AHS Class
of 2001 and several anti-bullying groups—that was
rich).

Sue clicked on the AHS group and was
bombarded by uploaded pictures of her most
detested classmates; the jocks and preppies, teeth
white and straight because Mommy and Daddy
could afford braces during their formative years.
They all wore identical expressions of smugness,
secure in the knowledge that they were the chosen
ones who would all get laid after prom, go off to

state universities, and marry a model mate and propagate more gigantic asshats.

She scrolled through the pictures and towards the end was shocked to see one that showed her sitting alone underneath the stairs. It was hard to miss the greasy carrot orange hair that hung in her eyes, her pale ankles peeking out from under her high-water jeans, and her muted face dotted with red, oozing pimples. She had been a real pizza face back then, no matter how much Noxzema she used. Her head was bent over a book that prominently displayed a dragon breathing fire with a wizard astride it on the cover. One of the jocks had commented, only days before, "Look at Sue reading about her dwagons!"

The w in the word said it all—a conscious decision to mock her speech impediment. One of the jackoff's fried neurons must have piped up, "Hey you know what would be hilarious? If you put a 'w' instead of an 'r' in the word! Classic!"

Tears welled up, but she sniffled them back. Her chest filled with indignant heat…after twenty years? Still?

She clicked back to the main page for the reunion, taking in the details. To be held at the town's banquet hall, cash bar, and the food catered by one of the hottest new restaurants in town, Pastasciutta. Just last week her mother's best friend sat at this very table and gushed about the restaurant, extolling the virtues of their pasta made in-house every night and she'd capped her review with, "the tiramisu was better than any sex I've ever had, honest to God!". Her mother had been deep into her wine bottle by then, her eyes glassy and dreamy, but she'd offered up the requisite chuckle at her friend's statement.

A pleasant buzz crept up her neck, making her head swim in a tranquil manner. Ah, the Xanax kicking in.

Sue zoned out, her eyes unfocused, staring out the large kitchen window that looked out to the front yard. She absently gazed at the flower beds that were budding with green stems. None had yet bloomed but if the weather held—she could expect to be greeted by bobbing pink and yellow tulips. The dark green glossy leaves of the oleander waved in the breeze. Soon the white flowers would burst open and add a nice splash of color to the yard.

Hard to believe such a lovely plant could be so deadly.

She frowned—and then a slow smile crept up, and, in that moment, she felt achingly beautiful. She surely looked the part of a Greek goddess or some Victorian noble overlooking their garden.

The leaves beckoned her, dancing merrily with each gust of wind.

Chapter Two

On a whim, she made a reservation for herself at Pastasciutta the next night.

Table for one.

She briefly considered asking her mother if she wanted to join, but the only thing more pathetic than eating alone was dining with your wine addled, eccentric mother. She'd served as an endless source of irritation and embarrassment for Sue as she grew up; always showing up to school events dressed in styles that had been hip thirty years ago, and she had a penchant for shiny, clunky jewelry that clanged with her every movement. Like a crow hoarding glittering treasures. Her soft blue eyes bulged behind the lenses of oversized glasses that had long fallen out of fashion. She waxed philosophical about the star signs, always greeting any piece of bad news with, "Well… Mercury *is* in retrograde" as if this mere fact explained why the world was going to hell in a handbasket.

Mercury was always in retrograde, according to her mother.

Seeing her in public always made Sue think of a beautiful, ostracized butterfly in the midst of uniformly gray moths.

Add her mother to the list of reasons she was an outsider at school. *"Hey Sue, think your Mom will let me fuck her doggy style? I'll even wear a tie-dye condom and I'll bring my healing crystals!"*

Sue entered the restaurant, already clutching

her purse for dear life with whitened knuckles and sweaty palms. She waited at the ornate wooden stand to be seated. Carved leaves and vines adorned the wood. Glittering chandeliers hung from the ceiling, filling the large dining room with soft yellow light that likely served to make the food more appetizing. The light had the added bonus of making all the patrons appear more beautiful and elegant than they actually were. Pictures of smiling peasant women stomping grapes in giant vats lined the walls. Each table was topped with a pressed linen cloth and was set with a dazzling variety of silverware.

She took in the opulence. *Best look up which fork to use on my phone, so I don't look like an uncultured yokel.*

A thin mustached man in a simple black evening jacket sauntered up to her, bowing ever so slightly at the hips, as if he were greeting minor royalty, not a queen but perhaps a duchess. No doubt the jacket was painstakingly crafted by a tailor's delicate hands and cost more than her car.

"Good evening, miss. Might you have a reservation?" He spoke with efficiency and a hint of an accent, European of some sort. Likely Italian, since this was a pasta place after all. The only Italians that Sue was familiar with were from *The Sopranos* and this gentleman looked much more polished than Tony Soprano. He probably wouldn't bust her kneecaps, either.

Probably not.

"Table for one, under Moore." She was careful to speak slowly, forming the words in her mind before saying them out loud. Her speech had improved significantly from her school days when her tongue got caught like a skipping record on "s" sounds and her "r's" came out as "w's". A rather cruel joke was that her full name included both of her trouble letters.

God had a fucked-up sense of humor.

"Right this way, miss." The maître d bent his elbow, clearly intending that she take his arm while he escorted her to her lonely table for one. A blush rose on her cheeks as she accepted his offered arm. She felt a bit foolish at the gesture but also relished the small crumb of human contact he extended towards her.

He stopped, pulling out her chair, then placed a neat linen napkin on her lap once she was seated. He steepled his thin, long fingers and gave her a little bow. Turning sharply with the grace of a dancer, he spirited away to regions unknown—perhaps out to the back alley to sneak a cigarette in preparation for a long night of impeccable manners and admonishing the wait staff.

She gazed at the guttering candle in the middle of her table, watching the shadows it tossed on the white tablecloth. She clutched her small purse in her hands, kneading the material in her fingers, comforted like a child would be with a favorite blanket.

"Hello there, miss. I will be your waiter tonight; my name is Mauricio." A deep voice to her left jerked her out of her reverie, grounding her in the here and now. She glanced at the voice's owner and her stomach flipped nervously at the sight of him.

He was olive skinned with a thatch of thick black hair that was combed back. A renegade curl twisted down his forehead, making him seem somewhat boyish and adding to his handsome looks. Bright green eyes twinkled at her, sparkling like brilliant emeralds when the candlelight caught them just right. His lips were Cupid-bowed and a perfect shade of pink. He regarded her for a moment before breaking out in a beaming smile, revealing gleaming white teeth. The expression, rather than putting her at ease, instead made her internal temperature rise by twenty degrees.

Scorching.

"What can I start you out with? A bottle of wine, or perhaps the lady would like to try our famous sangria?" His lips twitched in amusement and he lowered his voice, leaning in conspiratorially close to her ear, "We also have a very nice Diet Coke. The best in town."

The giggles escaped her mouth before she knew it, barreling out with reckless abandon. She brought both her hands up to stifle the outburst, then turned the laughter down to a chuckle that soon petered off. The rolling of her stomach vanished with his little joke and she found herself able to make eye contact with the striking man. "I'll take the Diet Coke, if you please."

"Very good choice, miss. We have a variety of

specials tonight, unless you have something already in mind?"

Like any true obsessive, she'd agonized over the menu in the relative comfort of her home. She had recited her order over and over again until she could say it without a hint of stutter. "I would like to try your house-made spaghetti with meatballs. I would also like to try one of your charcuterie boards, but without any nuts. I'm horribly allergic." She smiled sheepishly at him, feeling like she always did when she told anyone of her allergy—a bit defective, as if an essential human part of her had been misplaced during her making.

His glittering green eyes widened, and his thick black eyebrows arched up, "Of course, miss. I will tell them about your allergy and if you see a nut within 10 feet of this table, I will deal with it harshly." He clenched his hand into a fist and smacked it in the other hand. "One Diet Coke coming up!"

She watched him move lithely to the kitchen and realized she had been clutching her purse with the intensity of a drowning man clasping a life preserver. Unclenching her fingers with an effort, she fanned them out, working out the cramp that was threatening to settle within. She instead unclasped her red purse, fetching out a Chapstick, then applied a thin coat to her dry lips. Her fingers brushed along the thick plastic casing of her Epi-Pen at the bottom of the bag, next to a pack of Juicy Fruit gum and a bundle of forgotten receipts.

Mauricio came back with a glass of Diet Coke, setting it on the table. "Anything else for you while you wait, miss?"

She started to shake her head no, ready to dismiss him, but her mouth opened unbidden. "I wanted to ask—does your restaurant cater events?"

He nodded and took a deep inhale before

exclaiming, "Yes, of course! We need advance notice obviously, but we can make anything on our menu for any event. Our chef makes everything in-house, and we partner with a local catering company to ensure the food gets to its destination as intended—proper presentation is part of a great meal, as you well know." He said this last bit with a hint of arrogance, as if a properly set dinner table might send him into raptures of delight.

"How much notice do you need? Does the chef cook the food in advance and then—freeze it?"

A wounded look entered his eyes, and the dazzling green color shifted into a muddled blue. He put his hand to his chest, as if he had been shot directly in the heart, "My God, no! We do not freeze any of our dishes, to do so would dilute their taste. Our chef cooks everything that day, or that night before. Only the freshest, most quality food comes from our kitchen."

She suspected that he just might give someone the Tony Soprano treatment if they violated these basic commandments of cooking and food preparation. A crowbar right across the kneecaps, followed by a satisfying crack as the bone splintered.

She shrugged, embarrassed to have offended him so much on the subject. "Ah, I understand now. Sorry, I am not familiar with gourmet cuisine. I'm trying to…" she picked up her glass of Diet Coke and made as if to toast him, "broaden my horizons. Thank you for helping me." She forced a smile, the gesture unnatural on her face, but his eyes immediately softened.

"No problem, miss! Feel free to ask me anything at all. I am here only to serve you. But I do believe I see your charcuterie board up. Let me fetch it for you!"

She relaxed in her seat, sagging backwards

into the thick cushioning. Mauricio triumphantly presented the appetizer to her, proudly proclaiming, "And not one nut in sight, miss!"

Her Epi-Pen sat at the bottom of her bag, unused during her authentic Italian dinner.

True to Mauricio's word, there was not one nut in sight.

Chapter Three

Sue tumbled into bed, her stomach satiated, with a lingering aftertaste of garlic in her mouth. The strong garlic overwhelmed the Colgate and brilliant green (just like Mauricio's eyes) mouthwash. Bedcovers enveloped her, making her feel safe and cocooned like a caterpillar getting a head start on its transformation to a butterfly. Unfortunately, she never woke up as someone different, just her plain, boring self. She nestled her head into the pillow and listened to the trees rustling outside her window, their branches budding out more new leaves every day.

Her breathing slowed into a steady, deep rhythm and she was spirited away to the land of dreams—and nightmares.

She sits like an omnipotent God, watching the drama unfold in front of her. She might as well be seated in a theater chair, rolling the program tightly into a tube with fidgeting hands. Except—she also sees *everything* and feels *everything* all the players onstage experience. She resides in the brains of all the performers and is privy to their emotions, their thoughts, their dreams—everything that might have crossed their mind at one time or another.

She's seated at the end of one of the red tables in the cafeteria—alone, as always, with a book in hand. A cacophony of noise litters the air; excited shouts of students that haven't seen each other for hours and greet each other like they'd been lost at sea for years; the screeches of lunch trays sliding on metal, a noise that makes teeth fillings ache; and a symphony of bags zipping open and shut. The story of her book draws her in, transporting her light years away from an ordinary school day, and plops her down in a meadow where sprites with gossamer wings swirl about, beckoning the hero further on in his quest.

She is so engrossed in the plot she notices nothing around her, but at the same time, in her omnipotent throne, she sees all. *She doesn't glimpse with her eyes the jocks two tables away having a milk chugging contest, their orange letterman jackets now a darker rust colored shade, fortified with a healthy portion of calcium.*

They don't care that there are starving children in Africa.

She doesn't see Lauren Georgia walking towards her table, an evil glint in her eye and her face held in a supremely smug smirk. She flicks her gaze around, meeting eyes bright with gay humor. Sue's head is bent over, her nose only inches from the fold of the book, and all she sees is a green meadow where a babbling brook provides water to a parched hero.

The voyeur Sue of now *discerns everything, though; she resides in the jocks' stomachs bulging with milk, and she lives in Lauren's head and is privy to her machinations. She screams at her reading self, begging her to look up and "pay attention" but her words fall on deaf ears. No one looks about, trying to puzzle out the warning from nowhere.*

Lauren swipes the sandwich that Sue brought from home—a honey and banana sandwich—and exchanges it with a peanut butter and jelly sandwich. She makes the original sandwich disappear, as quickly as a Vegas dealer would make your chips from a losing bet vanish.

Poof, gone.

Lauren glances around her, a cruel, upturned smile dominating her face. It obscures her features, making her look less a beauty queen and more a caricature of a monster. All that is needed to complete the ensemble would be a few expertly placed warts and some curved yellow horns jutting out from her smooth, acne-free forehead. All those that she makes eye contact with are in on the joke, and they look at her with a variety of expressions; a mix of pure adulteration, mean spirited mischievousness, and others with an undercurrent of guilt—not that they will for one second try to stop the show.

Sue gropes for her sandwich in front of her, too engrossed in her book to drop her gaze. She doesn't even look before taking a huge bite and chewing mechanically. Her taste buds don't ring any alarm bells at the change from honey to jelly—sugar is sugar to them—but her brain registers a change in texture while she swallows. The peanut butter sticks to the roof of her mouth and her eyes widen with alarm.

Peanut butter? Oh fuck.

She glances down at her hands and already they are on fire, a blotchy rash blooming over the backs of them like a wildfire devouring prairie grass on a hot, still day, growing before her very eyes. An intense burning itch greets her nerves and other areas of her body flare into being, the same rash taking up residence there. The skin under her bra straps prickles with an intensity that begs for her nails to scratch, scratch, scratch—drawing blood if necessary.

Anything to stop the maddening itch!

Her nose switches on like a faucet, clear snot running down her face and onto her lips—lips that are already ballooning. She tries to swallow again, her throat dry, but finds that her mouth is dominated by the alarming bulk of her bloated tongue.

No wiggle-room.

Small indentations ring the tip of her graying tongue, pinpricks of blood welling up in each of them—her crooked (and oddly sharp) teeth are helpless, betraying their master by cutting into the swelling flesh. Her mouth gapes open like a dog panting, and she tries taking a breath (a remarkable feat when you only have a millimeter of clearance from your tongue and the roof of your mouth).

Her throat is raw, like she's spent hours screaming at the tops of her lungs and what little breath she draws down it is ragged and hitching. Her heart races, thrumming into overdrive, her body spills out stress hormones which only fuel her growing anxiety and fear. Nostrils flaring, she smells a sour odor that she realizes is coming from her.

It's the smell of pure, unadulterated panic.

A faint wheeze reaches her ears, unrecognizable as a sound a human being might make, but it's air coming out of the pinhole she used to call a throat.

She lunges for her backpack, scrambling to find the Epi-Pen she carries everywhere with her for emergencies.

For just in case.

Just in case has arrived in spectacular fashion, and where is that damn pen? *Her blind fingers fumble, closing around highlighters, pens, and a TI-84 calculator—no Epi-Pen.*

She tries to take a deep breath, tries to calm herself, but her throat has swollen shut and no air enters. Her eyes water, streaming salty tears down her face that mingle with the cascade of snot from her nose. Bright red hives erupt on her eyelids and cause her skin to swell, reducing her visual field to a mere slit. Involuntarily, she clutches at her throat, clawing with fingers that have hooked into talons. Skin cells take residence underneath her fingernails, soon to be joined by blood drawn forth by her nails.

Her face is puffy, blotched in red, but a tinge of blue creeps around the edges of her lips. The beginnings of cyanosis—the proverbial white flag of a body declaring itself deprived of oxygen.

One of the cafeteria workers, a slight lady named Regina, looks up then. She was woolgathering, thinking of how many more shifts she'll need to work to afford a new set of tires for her car, which are balder than Mr. Clean. She registers the jeering laughter of kids—the type of laughter and riotous yelling that can only be associated with someone else's suffering.

Kids really were the fucking worst.

She scans the lunchroom and instantly sees the quiet girl that always sits alone, clutching her throat in the universal sign of choking. Her body reacts before her mind can. She launches away from her spot in the cafeteria line, where today she is slopping meatloaf onto waiting trays. She runs flat out, pushing aside a group of chortling assholes who point and giggle at the ailing girl.

"Hey, watch it!" One of the jerk-offs yells, rubbing a sore hip, fresh from a collision with a table. She pays him no heed, her arms pumping up and down as she cuts the distance between her and the girl.

Sue's eyes are bulging in their sockets, staring blindly around the lunchroom since the skin of her eyelids has nearly cut off her field of vision completely. Her remaining sliver of vision has blacked out at the edges and she can only make out grayish figures swimming about her. They too will *soon be obliterated by the all-encompassing black that is threatening to overwhelm her. Her nails tear into her throat, drawing blood that wells up from the scratches, an animal instinct spurning her on, telling her to open up her own throat to survive.*

Regina stops in front of her, taking in the nightmarish scene that has unfolded before her. The poor girl is one big hive, her lips grotesquely bloated, like a socialite with lip injections gone wrong. A frightening rasp comes from her throat— trying to talk or trying to breathe? At first, Regina thought the girl had choked on food, but it's much worse than that. The Heimlich won't do shit to resolve this situation. The girl is having an allergic reaction—anaphylaxis—and she's dying right in front of everyone and all these assholes can do is point and laugh?

"Do you have an Epi-Pen?"

The dying girl takes a moment from tearing at

her throat and shakily points at the floor, at her backpack. Regina dives for it, upending all the contents. Spiral notebooks splay open, loose papers scatter, and pens clatter. Regina gives the bag one hefty shake, and the prize flies out.

The girl's Epi-Pen.

They didn't cover this in orientation, focusing more on the Heimlich and proper handwashing technique, but her younger brother was deathly allergic to bees. Her mother schooled her on the Epi-Pen, putting her through paces until she could administer it blindfolded. She slides the pen out of its case.

Blue to the sky, orange to the thigh, *she recites to herself. She jams the orange tip to the girl's thigh and then clicks down, holding it for a count of 3.* One-Mississippi, two-Mississippi, three-Mississippi.

Sue slumps over, losing consciousness then,

the skin of her face taking on an alarming hue of blue. Her hives appear to have diminished but really are masked by the duskiness overwhelming her skin. Regina cradles her in her arms and screams, "Someone call 911, for fuck's sake!" Her scream echoes back to her ears, doubling, trebling, magnified by the cafeteria's acoustics. Oddly blank faces peer at the spectacle, some with tears tracking down their faces—not in distress, but the type of tears produced from laughing so hard that your sides ache and you gasp for air—not unlike poor Sue.

Seeing such a horde so content, positively fucking thrilled to watch another die in front of them—it's not hard to see why monsters such as Nazis rose to power.

A mousy girl, Kristyn Moon, far in the back, peels away from the jubilant crowd, her trance broken by Regina's shouted command. Kristyn started kindergarten with Sue, often sitting just a desk away owing to alphabetical seating charts. The two had shared sticks of gum through the years, and while Sue was a bit weird, Kristyn had always liked her. Theirs was an easy companionability born of forced shared proximity. All the same—Kristyn found herself swept up by the rabble, the infectious malice that permeated the air with its stink, that intoxicated everyone it touched with its rotting finger. Part of her yearned to watch the life ebb away from another, was positively enraptured by the idea. Kristyn who demanded that her father capture a spider under a glass and release it to the safety of their backyard, Kristyn who cried every damn time the dog died in Old Yeller, that very same Kristyn let waves of pleasure roll over her watching the suffering of a classmate who once shyly smiled before offering her a stick of Juicy Fruit. Her fingers shake as she dials 9-1-1, not because she is fearful for Sue's fate but because the comedown from a dopamine flood is a real bitch.

Sue gasped, her chest heaving for breath, dried tears on her cheeks. Her fingers were wrapped around her throat and she felt the warm outline of her scar, her souvenir of that horrible day. Her body had been blissfully unaware of what was happening to her, having been starved of oxygen for so long. All its critical systems had shut down, except for the centers that controlled her heartbeat.

Later, she heard all about how the paramedics had kept jabbing her full of more Epinephrine, draining their supply on the ambulance with barely a reduction in the swelling of her lips and tongue.

Then, a doctor in the ER had taken one look at her mouth and realized trying for an endotracheal tube would be folly and instead, took a scalpel to her throat, opening up a hole to allow lifesaving air in.

A cric, they called it.

Her throat felt abraded like it had that day—before it swelled shut. Each intake of air felt like nails had been hammered in, embedded in the tissue, raking her with each inhalation.

She brought her knees up, hugging them to her chest and threw the sheets off of her. They were hopelessly twisted, untucked from the corners of the bed, and sweat soaked.

The nightmare used to come nightly, sometimes even twice or three times a night, slowly picking away at her sanity. How long could someone last against a nightmare like that? And for years on end? She'd suffered for ten years!

She'd tried everything, drugging herself with Benadryl before sleep, which only gave the nightmare a dreamier quality and caused her to feel hungover in the morning. Alcohol worked better, causing her to black out. But after a while, her tolerance grew, and she could no longer drink enough to prevent the nightmare from coming. It also worried her when she got to where she *had* to drink to stop her limbs from shaking during the day. She didn't exactly want to follow in her dear mother's footsteps.

A perfect solution to the nightmare? Why, quit sleeping altogether, obviously; rationalizing that if she was awake, she wouldn't have to live through that day again and again. It was like Groundhog Day, except without the cute little critter and the charming antics of Bill Murray.

The not sleeping worked—for a while. That is until it triggered a psychotic break, fracturing all she held near and dear. The big whoops, as she liked to think of it, had convinced her she would be better off dead, and she'd nearly kept her appointment with the Grim Reaper.

He'd been heartily upset that she escaped his clutches that day in the cafeteria.

Her brain became deluged with hallucinations of her high school tormentors. Their faces would undulate around her head, their mouths moving in horrid approximations of laughter. Their tongues would poke out, forked at the ends, and their skin would crawl with bloated white bugs that would occasionally rear a blank black face at her. These images accompanied her through all her waking moments, bombarding her already fragile psyche.

A solution came to her, breaking through the swirling deliriums that had come to dominate her life.

The final solution.

She'd locked herself in the bathroom and drew a hot bath. She lit candles around the tub, taking small pleasure in the flickering flames.

It was harder to see the faces in candlelight,

although oddly enough, far easier to see them in the pitch blackness of her bedroom in the early morning hours when she lay stark awake, cowering. A full bottle of aspirin waited for her by the tub, specially purchased for this last night. How fucking ridiculous was it that this stuff was sold over the counter, as if it were a benign entity?

She stripped naked, her pale skin reddening in the hot water. The childproof cap was far too easy to remove, and she shook five tablets out at time into her sweat-slickened palm, tossing them in her mouth—like peanuts you might get at a bar—then washed them back with a slug of red wine. She repeated this until the bottle was empty and her head was swimming, boozed up from all the wine. The room took on a dreamy quality that didn't feel real. Sputtering shadows danced along the tile, and she closed her eyes, succumbing to the siren call of sleep that the wine and aspirin promised her.

Her venture was ultimately unsuccessful.

There was a joke in there somewhere; how do you know you're a failure? You can't even kill yourself!

The miracle, as told by her mother , was that either a higher power had intervened or it was a stroke of luck (good or bad, depending on one's perspective). The shower curtain must've fluttered about, possibly set into motion by her hand grazing it, or perhaps an errant breeze wafting through the bathroom at an (in)opportune time? Either way, a hungry flame licked the curtain, at first smoldering, then spectacularly catching it alight. The orange flame dashed upwards and outwards, producing a thick black smoke that went unnoticed by Sue.

The unconscious weren't renowned for their superb sense of smell.

Just Desserts

Tendrils of smoke tickled the bathroom's smoke detector, spurning the device to emit high-pitched shrieks that made dogs a block over howl in pain. The screeching brought her mother running and, finding the door locked, she'd lowered her shoulder and charged through, splintering the door on its frame and gaining admittance to the bathroom.

Sue roused some, achieving a level consistent with dreamy somnolence. The crashing sounds had penetrated her haze. Her head was splitting with a headache (which was impressive in itself, with all that aspirin in her system), her eyes were half-mast and sleepy, and she mumbled, "Wassssamatta?"

Her mother had thrown bathwater on the curtain, extinguishing the blaze. She'd then taken in the empty bottle of aspirin, the drained glass of wine, and Sue slumped and muttering unintelligibly in a heap, and completed the macabre math equation with ease. She hauled her daughter out of the tepid bathwater and onto the faded bathmat. Sue's skin felt wrinkled, like she'd aged decades in that bathtub. Her mother had wrapped a plush towel around her daughter's shaking shoulders and dialed 911, saving Sue's life.

A week of her life was spent in a twilight of intermittent consciousness only enjoyed by the critically ill in comas or by those hooked up to sedative drips. Sue was a blend of the two; part of her brain was dim from a lack of glucose as a consequence of the aspirin poisoning, something she read about later. A glass vial of stark white medicine, Propofol—milk of amnesia—dripped steadily into her IV, acting to keep her mostly sedated.

Monitors beeped with regularity around her and the air smelled medicinal—of gauze and fresh bandages. People dressed in pale green scrubs would periodically shine bright lights directly into her eyeballs, prying her eyelids open no matter how hard she squeezed them shut. Part of her ICU stay was spent hooked up to a dialysis machine that acted like a peripheral kidney, cleaning her blood of the toxin she had force fed it. She didn't remember much about that except for the whirring of the machine as it worked, a nice white noise that was pretty soothing, truth be told.

Various tubes snaked into all her bodily orifices, some dripping in medication, while others shuttled waste away. As time went on, more of the tubes were removed. Shifting in the bed revealed a tube that was threaded into her urethra, colored amber by her urine. She was very nervous to move after this discovery, imagining the terrible ripping sensation that would occur if she dislodged this precarious tube.

After a doctor came in one morning, proclaiming her, "Medically cleared!" another doctor came trudging in on his heels. This doctor didn't have a stethoscope looped around his shoulders like the others, and his right middle finger bore a calloused bump that only came from a career of feverish writing.

A psychiatrist then.

He introduced himself as Dr. Young and, using words rather than the usual sharp implements, started probing at her softer, vulnerable parts. She remained tightlipped, not answering any of his intrusive questions, which caused him to emit a sigh coupled with a shake of his head. His hair didn't move at all, making her wonder if it was a piece or if he had sprayed it into submission with generous heaps of Aqua Net. As a rule, psychiatrists didn't get within six feet of their patients, so she was unable to catch any scent of hairspray in the air.

"My dear, I'm afraid we are going to have to get you professional help." He said this softly and clearly wanted her to think it pained him to do so, but she wasn't fooled. His eyes lit up as he said it— her fucked up mind would probably bankroll his second vacation home. She rolled her eyes and a cloud of displeasure crossed his face, gone as quickly as it came, replaced by a thin smile.

Chapter Four

S ue shook her head vigorously and attacked her eyes with the heels of her hands. Brilliant stars kaleidoscoped behind her closed eyes. Her eyelids opened slowly, her vision bleary. The room was dark with lurking shadows that made her shiver, although she'd long since learned the real monsters are the people who walk around every day with human masks pulled over their insidious features.

The nightmare came less frequently, but when it did, it caused her to remember all the low points in her short life. She let out a sigh.

Guess it's time to get up then.

Her back cracked as she threw the damp covers off the bed. Her feet found their home in bunny slippers, then she padded down the hall to the kitchen.

The house was quiet except for the occasional creak of it settling—although Sue wasn't convinced there weren't ghosts roaming about. An empty bottle of wine laid on its side on the counter—a party favor from her mother's night. Two purple drops clung to the countertop, threatening to stain. A slow night then. Usually, her mom could put away at least two bottles alone. Champion liver, that one. Her sleep was probably much more restful than Sue's.

Her mind was disengaged, but her body moved of its own accord. Hands heaped scoop after scoop of ground coffee into the filter. Her nostrils flared, taking in the rich aroma. She filled the pot with cold water and started the contraption, relishing the clicking noise that signaled the caffeine would soon hit her blood stream. She was careful to keep her mind as blank as possible, instead focusing on her breathing and the movement of her diaphragm with each breath in and out.

In... and out.

One of the counselors she was paired up with during her "vacation" at the psych hospital made her realize she was suffering from PTSD. The idea sounded absurd to Sue. She hadn't fought in a war where bombs dropped from the sky, and she hadn't pulled a trigger or killed anyone. She didn't hyperventilate when helicopters flew overhead or become stock still every time a car backfired in the streets.

"Sue, you have to realize that your trauma is as valid and true as any other trauma anyone else has experienced. Once you can accept that, you can start the journey of healing."

Sounded like some new age baloney bullshit to her. She sat each day in the chair across from him, closed off, letting the minutes run out until she could return to her cell—oh no, her *room*. Her gray room that had thick black bars on the window, allowing only snatches of sunlight to shine in on the equally drab floor. Her roommate was a real nutso too, sporting haunted eyes which burned like black coals when she looked at Sue. Thick smudges that looked like bruises had taken up permanent residence under those cursed eyes. The woman was a new mother who suffered from debilitating postpartum depression, whose husband thwarted an attempt to drown her newborn baby girl in the bath.

An Andrea Yates wannabe.

A real psycho—not like Sue.

Sue's hair always hung in her face during

those therapy visits, in greasy strips that obscured her vision. She kept her gaze on her feet and her cuticles were chewed ragged and took on a reddish-purple tinge, looking like infection would bloom from them at any time. She attacked them with her teeth until she drew blood, finding an odd comfort in inflicting pain on herself.

Each day, her therapist tried to ply her with soothing words, speaking in that tone of voice one used around the clinically insane, profoundly mentally disabled, or a scared animal backed into a corner. His words held no meaning for her, and a breakthrough seemed a long time coming. She had withdrawn into herself, content to bide her time until they released her and she could try her hand at suicide again. This time she wouldn't fuck it up— she would succeed and end the pain once and for all, giving way to nothingness. Unless you were Catholic and believed that committing suicide punched you a one-way ticket to Hell. Luckily Sue considered herself agonistic verging on atheist, so such beliefs didn't trouble her any.

The coveted breakthrough came one day with no warning. The same soothing "talking to animals and idiots" voice had failed to invoke a reaction, so her therapist tried something completely different.

Physical touch.

With a gentle pressure of a finger under her chin. he tilted her head up so she could look at him, truly look at him. The worried compassion in his pale blue eyes broke her, causing her to cry ugly, hitching sobs—if she was in her room with her wacko roomie, they probably would have sedated her.

She'd exhausted her store of tears with him that day. It was like a dam had burst; a dam that had been holding back poisonous water that was festering, absolutely teeming with noxious creatures. It was all too easy to imagine the creatures too; spiny fish with razor-sharp teeth, blind white eyes bloated like skinned grapes; translucent worms with thick venomous pincers. Each of them whispering, *"Sue, just do it, try killing yourself again. This time, inject yourself with insulin in the woods! They'll never find you and you'll get the job done!"* All the creatures, gone and released, returned to the wild—or Hell.

With her therapist's help, she started working on coping mechanisms and moving past all the wrongs; the taunts, the teases, and the outright homicidal actions of her peers. She made her mental health a priority; practicing "mindfulness" where she cleared her mind, focused on her breathing and becoming one with the universe.

Weeks after her breakthrough, she was released from the locked down psych ward, buzzed through the doors by a fat, surly looking nurse, waving a companionable goodbye to her wretched roommate who tried in vain to drown her new daughter.

After that?

Weekly visits with another therapist who seemed intent on uncovering some sort of molestation plot in her past; and imbibing a rainbow of pills that helped her restore some normalcy to her fucked up brain chemistry.

Things seemed… better?

But with the recurrence of that dream, the re-living of it all, she might have to rethink the granola "just move past all the bullshit" way of thinking.

Over and over, she was extolled on the virtues of forgiveness. First in the psych ward during their group sessions led by a wispy, hippie looking woman who looked like she could use a hefty dose of Haldol herself, then by her therapist, who seemed convinced she had been molested by a handsy uncle.

Their sermons all contained gems that sounded like they had been stolen from motivational posters showing a cat hanging off of a clothesline; "To forgive is to set a prisoner free and discover that the prisoner was you"; "Forgive others not because they deserve forgiveness but because you deserve peace", and the most vomit inducing, "Forgiveness is a gift you give yourself.".

A little voice started whispering to her after her release, its tone seductive and low, almost a purr, and the suggestions it made—were persuasive!

Revenge.

What was better than living well?

Revenge.

What was better than forgiveness?

Revenge.

The silky voice made her arms erupt in goosebumps, made the back of her skull buzz with excitement, made her feel fuckin' alive for once in her life.

How could she resist the siren call?

The voice supplied another quote to her, one surely not plastered on a poster showing a tranquil mountain range ringed within a calming morning mist. The voice was low and had a hissing quality to it, like a snake thrusting its tongue out into the air.

Hissssss.

Not unlike her speech impediment.

It spoke, creating dimpled gooseflesh that caused her pale arm hairs to stand on end, sounding as if it was whispering in her ear, its breath sending awful yet pleasurable tingles down her spine. "Sooner or later, everyone sits down to a banquet of consequences."

A banquet—nicely catered.

Chapter Five

S ue sat in the dark kitchen, having neglected to flick the light switches to *on*, clutching her mug (pasted on the front was The Honorable Ruth Bader Ginsburg flipping a double bird, *Dissent* stamped underneath the great Justice), and whiled away the time on her laptop, reading fan fiction. The clock hands ticked by with petulant slowness, each minute lasting hours. *Why are scientists trying to manipulate time when I can do it so easily?*

The obnoxious cuckoo clock in the living room erupted at 8:00 AM, screaming out eight consecutive cuckoos before going back into its hidey hole, marshaling its strength for the next hour's screaming.

It's a wonder that fucking thing didn't drive me nuts first, instead I had to wait for my asshole classmates to do it.

Still, the bird's conniption signaled it was time for a visit to the public library.

The old maid manning the front desk waved at Sue, peering at her over half-moon glasses that usually dangled by a thin silver chain between her wasted bosoms. She spoke with a reedy, high voice that sounded breathless, like she maybe needed a good rest and a nice glass of Ovaltine.

"Sue! We got in a shipment of those 'Warriors' books—you know, the ones with the talking cats—"

"Oh, that's okay Mildred, I'll have to look those up next time. I have some other stuff to take care of today."

"No problem, enjoy yourself!" Mildred flapped a hand, her frail bones filling the air with a faint creaking noise. Maybe Miss Mildred ought to add calcium supplements to her grocery list in addition to some tasty Ovaltine.

Sue meandered in the stacks rather than gravitating towards the fantasy section where the books boasted a full complement of knights, wizards, orcs—the shit that really got her going. Instead, she passed them up—reluctantly. A junkie always feels pangs of despair when they forgo their preferred fix—and located the section labeled "gardening".

She skimmed the spines of the books, running a finger along the vertical titles, not knowing exactly what she was looking for, but confident the title would reveal itself. *Gardening for Dummies, How Plants Saved My Life* (hard pass on that), *Succulents Don't Suc!* (how witty, Sue wished the author a painful, protracted bout with a large, pointed kidney stone), and—yes—*Common Plants as Poisons.* She glanced both ways down the aisle before grabbing the book and ushering it to an unoccupied table in the corner.

At the early hour, the library was relatively empty. Only she and an elderly man wearing headphones that were probably manufactured in 1960 sat at the tables. Every sound was magnified by the emptiness, each sneeze and flutter of pages sounding as if it was being blasted from a set of speakers. The old man peered at a large book full of pictures with a magnifying glass. His rheumy blue eye looked gigantic behind the glass. *Can't hear and can't see worth a shit, bummer.*

She opened the book, wincing as the spine

cracked—a cardinal sin in the eyes of book lovers everywhere—and scanned the table of contents. She thumbed through to her desired section and read the words that unspooled across the pages with her head bent over, completely absorbed in the details of her book. Had her eyes not been flickering to and fro, she looked the part of a woman lost in prayer.

The elderly man glanced up, one of the joints in his neck giving a terrific and satisfying *crack*; taking a well-deserved break from looking at his book, *Pinups Through the Decades*. He liked using the magnifying glass because sometimes he could catch a hint of areola that would otherwise be missed. He thought the library's only other patron looked radiant, lost in her reading; her face feverish and bright with a smile that spread from ear to ear.

She must be in love, smiling like that.

He felt a squeeze in his heart, remembering the pangs of young love, back in the dinosaur age of long-ago. Either that or his angina was acting up. He thumbed out a glass vial from the pocket of his plaid shirt and popped a nitro under his tongue—just in case.

After spending a fruitful few hours with the book, Sue retired to the public computers in the back of the library. There were six screens with accompanying monitors, lined up in rows of three, their backs facing each other. Sitting next to each computer was a placard listing the various rules.

1. Limit time to 30 minutes if there is a wait

2. Treat this computer as if it were your own, no food or drinks

3. Act as if your mother was monitoring your search history, no lewd sites!

She clicked on an icon stylized to look like a spy, which placed the browser on incognito mode but was under no illusions that this made her anonymous. It might make her movements a little harder to track, though, if someone's curiosity was piqued.

The biggest benefit of the library was they didn't require a personal login to access the internet. There were certain safeguards set on the computers, you couldn't just willy-nilly google "big titted babes" (the elderly gentleman had tried such a search this morning and was disappointed to be directed to some bird called, The blue-footed booby), but for the most part, you could surf to your heart's content.

Sue spent some time applying her newfound knowledge of poisons to her searches and a plan took shape in her mind, causing her stomach to flip-flop with flutters of excitement. The little voice sat mostly in silence, piping up only occasionally, offering helpful hints. Her fingers flew over the keyboard, the clacks coming so regularly, they almost sounded like they were pounding out the rhythm of a song.

A song titled *Sweet Revenge*.

Being a bit of a nerd, she jumped on the Bitcoin bandwagon early and had amassed a small fortune in digital money. The cache had been sitting in cyberspace, waiting for a rainy day, but now her interests dictated she used some of her hard earned moola.

Displayed on the screen was a Chinese herbal supplement store and the contents of said store were—*enlightening*. Had the computer's speakers been turned on, a tinny song usually heard in the background of a Chinese restaurant, piping inoffensively out of speakers mounted in the corners, would have played. Most of the supplements and products on the site were marketed for weight loss, a few for sexual staying power, others for longevity (in life, not in sex). But a subset had more nefarious uses. She loaded her cart with these.

One hundred and fifty people in my graduating class—one hundred and fifty should do it!

A few more clicks of her mouse and her shipment was confirmed, her precious cargo slated to arrive three days before the reunion!

One last piece of business before heading home to a planned lunch of tuna sandwiches, and to ensure her mother didn't choke to death on rancid wine vomit in her stupor—she logged into Facebook and RSVP'd to the reunion.

Bet your ass I'll be there. Wild horses couldn't drag me away.

A smile crossed her face again and once more, she ran a finger absently over the scar on her throat. The scar tissue rasped along the whorls and lines of the pad of her finger, comforting her and reminding her of *before*.

The sensation sent an electric thrill down her spine, causing her to shiver with pleasure.

A brown uniform clad man dropped off a box that required a signature. The heat outside persisted, as evidenced by the man's pale legs peering out from under the pair of brown shorts. The legs were finely shaped, even as pale as they were. With each step and twist, thick cords of muscle rippled. Yummy calves and quadriceps. Normally a specimen like this would have caused Sue to stammer and avert her gaze, but her heart had taken residence in her throat for a far different reason, and her body thrummed with excitement. All her nerves hummed, making her feel like a live wire was buried deep within her. Her hand shook some while she signed the name; Lauren Georgia-Smith.

One could never be too careful when ordering dietary supplements such as these. The delivery man didn't seem to notice her shaky scrawl or the anxiety rolling off of her in waves, instead he glanced at the thick row of oleander that had just started to bloom. Small white flowers strained towards the sunlight, begging petals on display, full and brilliant.

He grabbed the pen from her, his rough fingers brushing up against her own, causing her to pull back in alarm, but not before she felt a pleasurable jolt between her legs. The muscles of his forearm clenched as he clutched the pen and clipboard to his chest.

"Aren't those oleanders over there?" he asked, jutting his chin towards the plants lining the sidewalk.

Her tongue laid clumsily in her mouth, making her fear that speaking would cause a jumble of w's to spill out in place of hard r's, and she managed a nod and a weak smile that twitched the corners of her lips.

"Pretty plants, but nasty. My grandpa had a horse that filled up on those, not sure why because they're supposed to be bitter as hell but...he keeled over real quick. That stuff kills your heart, you know." He said this last bit conversationally, as if it was the most natural thing in the world to speak to total strangers about death flowers.

She kept her face neutral and nodded again, not trusting her traitorous tongue, not around the handsome UPS man.

"Welp, have a nice day, Mrs. Georgia-Smith." He turned and made his way down the sidewalk, pausing to glance at the oleander once more. He departed with a rueful shake of his head, no doubt thinking of a dying horse in his death throes, thrashing legs, wild, baleful eyes, and a foaming mouth.

She set the box next to a large coffee bean

grinder, expensive judging by the sleek metallic lines and unpronounceable French brand name printed on the front. A hammer with a blood red handle and a box of gallon sized Ziplock bags laid amidst other clutter on the kitchen table.

Sue pushed a stack of gossip rags (her mom's) off the table onto the neighboring chair to make room for her project. Some Guido from the show, Jersey Shore, stared at her up from the cover of one of the magazines as if he was in disbelief to be so carelessly tossed aside. "Gym, tan, laundry, motherfucker," she whispered, taking extra care to pronounce all the r's in "motherfucker". It was one of her favorite words, so she better say it correctly.

The Chinese herbal store really fucked the box up with tape, applying at least three layers on all the seams, ensuring a tight seal on her precious cargo. She hacked through the tape with a kitchen knife, nearly piercing her palm in her excitement.

Reaching inside the box, adrenaline redlined in her system, causing her heart to race and her forehead to break out in beads of sweat despite the relative cool of air conditioning. If she used her Epi-Pen now, her heart would probably explode.

She hoisted out a plastic bag filled to the brim with nuts. 180 to be exact, 30 more than she suspected she might need. She'd never been one to take needless chances. She peered down at them, amazed at how much they looked like mini coconuts, or maybe a pair of monkey balls, if they were shaved. Not that she knew what monkey balls looked like, but she could imagine.

Reverently, she grasped one, marveling at its rough surface between her fingers. The shell was a dark brown, mixed with veins of lighter browns. Lightweight too, lighter than a walnut of the same size.

She touched the shell with her bare hands but

hanging from her back pocket were a pair of blue nitrile gloves, similar to the ones the nurses wore in the ER when they threaded a gastric lavage tube down her esophagus and pumped her stomach empty of all that lovely aspirin she'd imbibed. She planned to use the gloves when handling the pale nut residing inside the harmless shell, unsure if peanut allergy conferred an allergy to exotic nuts, but now was not the time to throw caution to the wind. The hateful blue gloves brought to mind beeping monitors, medicinal smells, and the holier than thou look shared amongst all the medical staff.

I suppose that's my own fault, getting PTSD from damn hospital gloves.

Sue pulled on the hospital grade gloves, and grinned, making a fist with her right hand. "Might I shove my fist straight up your ass, Lauren? Don't worry, I'll be gentle." She laughed, her tone light and merry.

A pair of plastic goggles perched atop her head, the kind one would wear when mixing up random shit in the chemistry lab in high school under the watchful eye of a hungover science teacher. She pulled them down over her eyes, remembering when one of the jocks flung an acid they were working with directly into his eyes. He had not been wearing his safety goggles—no sir. Safety googles were for nerds and he'd loudly stated this on multiple occasions to all his seat mates. His anguished cries were both alarming and pleasing to her ears; he'd once called her a dog and barked at her across the quad. His squealing sounded just like an upset, constipated Chihuahua.

Who was the dog now?

It was a real shame afterwards; he couldn't see more than a few feet in front of him. The acid had fried the delicate tissue of his eyeballs, leaving them a milky color, pupils clouded over with scar tissue.

And the kicker? A pitcher that couldn't see a batter sure as shit wasn't gonna be throwing fastballs and screwballs and the college that had been sniffing around the budding athlete abruptly yanked his full ride scholarship away.

Safety first!

Sue spent the rest of her afternoon in the throes of mechanical efficiency. She worked in her own little assembly line, first cracking the thin husk of the shell away. Nestled within was a quarter-sized nut so innocent looking, it was downright cute! She then crammed the nuts together in one of the gallon-sized Ziplock bags that were scheduled for a date with the gnashing gears of the coffee bean grinder. The fine pale tan dust from *that* venture—looking like powdered peanut butter, a forbidden item in her household for obvious reasons—was safely stored in a plastic container.

She took special care not to touch her bare skin

with her gloved hands, worried that she might trigger another charming anaphylaxis adventure. Her Epi-Pen counted among the items strewn on the table, easily within reach.

Just in case.

A fine day's work! She tossed the goggles on the top rack of the dishwasher and stripped the gloves off with an eye watering *snap!* These were double bagged and thrown in the garbage can in the corner of the garage.

Be gone foul nut dust!

All the nut dust met its death at the hands of a scalding hot shower and copious scrubbing fueled by lavender scented body wash—one of the few body washes that didn't cause her skin to erupt into hives or develop scaly patches of eczema.

Only three days until the reunion and she was one busy bee. She planned to drive out to the mall— a place that had always terrified her.

The mall's target customer? The Lauren Georgias of the world. A place where smug teenagers covered head to toe in brand name clothing, sipped calorie laden Frappuccinos and tortured anyone that didn't conform to their particular values and styles. They ruled the hallowed halls of the food court and the jewelry slinging Claire's with an iron fist. But she had big plans for the reunion, and it wouldn't hurt to turn up sporting a nice, new outfit with a little make-up adorning her face.

Chapter Six

S ue spent the night before the reunion in a sleepless daze. Sleep eluded her, partially because of the excitement clouding her thoughts, but mostly, because her nerves felt like they were on a razor's edge. The minutes ticked by with agonizing slowness, the cuckoo clock's hourly screeches coming roughly once every century. She laid in her bed with the covers pulled up to her chin, head cradled on the pillow, staring up at the white popcorn encrusted ceiling.

Thinking. Wondering.

Many attempts were made at sleep, but the closing of her eyes met with stubborn resistance from her mind. Her eyelids would reopen no matter how fervently she tried to clamp them shut. It reminded her of old Looney Tunes cartoons where Tweety Bird would yank on Sylvester's eyelids and cause them to rebound open with a bang.

What a very rude little bird.

Still, she did achieve a semblance of sleep since her night was haunted by half-dreams. The dreams melted away like wax dripping from a candle, most experienced but not recalled in the waking hours other than the crowd favorite that always plagued her—the charming anaphylaxis nightmare.

In last night's version, Regina hadn't made it to her in time and she choked to death on her bloated, black tongue.

No matter.

Recalling this dream while the first streaks of sunlight touched the horizon only strengthened her resolve.

The cuckoo called out seven screeches. 7:00 AM. Sue's mother snorted in the room next door and heaved in her bed, before stilling again. Last night, she drank more than normal, and Sue didn't expect her up until sometime in the afternoon.

No time like the present.

She wrenched her tired body out of the inviting, warm covers.

Thrusting her arms above her head, she relished the satisfying crack of her elbows and shoulders. She heard a tick from downstairs as the coffeemaker in the kitchen kicked on. Soon the wafting aroma of Colombian brew would caress her olfactory nerves. Those Colombian beans had not met the acquaintance of the coffee grinder, *those* beans were already pre-ground at the quaint coffee shop across from the library.

She hopped into a steaming shower, soap kissing every pale pink surface, shampoo and conditioner lathered to high hell in her hair, and a razor sheering off every errant body hair. At the mall, her face was scrutinized with alarming detail and a stern Eastern European woman tweezed away a large portion of Sue's previously busy eyebrows—and unibrow—along with a startling amount of hairs that had taken up residence on her upper lip. Enough time had passed that the skin didn't smart when the hot water struck it, but she felt oddly naked, like a fluffy cat who suffered the indignity of being shaved due to matts and poor hygiene.

Recalling all the helpful tips the pink haired girl at the salon supplied her, she combed and teased her hair, until her formerly bushy mane was sleek and pin straight. Of course, she was aided by a contingent of expensive products tacked onto her bill. At least they smelled nice and they *did* tame her petulant snarls into obedience. She'd given the stylist free rein, only asking for a stylish cut and the girl obliged, cutting ratty inches off, and creating layers that framed her face. She could imagine a Hollywood starlet with the same cut on the cover of one of her mom's gossip rags.

So darn trendy!

Growing up, her hair had been a horrid carrot orange but over the years, had thankfully muted into more of an auburn. The pink haired beautician looked at her hair with envy saying, "You know, plenty of women pay good money for this color. Consider yourself lucky."

At the make-up counter, a chunky pale woman with jet black hair, a septum ring, and expertly applied smokey eyes, schooled the clueless Sue on the ins and outs of applying make-up. The whole ordeal felt like a secret ritual undertaken by a coven of witches during the full moon and finally, she had been taken into the fold. She recalled the gothic woman's advice and her hands moved without hesitation, recreating, reciting the old spells.

The woman looking back at her in the mirror was unrecognizable; Sue wouldn't go so far as to call herself gorgeous, so damaged was her self-esteem after years of ridicule, but someone in the fashion industry might gape at her beauty, their eyes drawn to her sharp cheekbones and "editorial" presence. They might promise this woman covers of elite fashion magazines and representation by all the finest agencies. A woman such as this could dine at a five-star restaurant in Paris wearing Givenchy, and men would fall all over themselves to offer a light for a cigarette perched between two slender, well-manicured fingers.

Yet another woman, this one with calves that bulged pleasingly with every step in her red-bottomed high heels, guided her with her costume—or outfit, rather. It was hard not to think of it as a costume, since it felt so ridiculous and foreign on her. Sue always was drawn towards practical clothing; jeans (cargo preferred, lots of pockets for her supplies), sweatshirts that obscured her figure, and tennis shoes (often the very same shoes that middle-aged women favored for Jazzercise classes).

Instead, the woman insisted that Sue try a myriad of dresses and, after much back and forth, they settled on a dainty black dress paired with wine red flats. Sue's trial of high heels nearly ended with a trip to the hospital, and a dull throb still stung the offending ankle joint. She had all the grace of a newborn giraffe, all gawky, gangly legs and no coordination. The outfit was completed with a simple pair of diamond stud earrings and a dangling necklace that plunged down to rest between her breasts. Breasts now enclosed in a brand spanking new bra and underwear set picked out by the nice saleswoman at Victoria's Secret. No more sports bras for Sue!

She looked in the full-length mirror outside her mother's bedroom.

Damn...I clean up alright, those assholes probably won't even recognize me!

The make-up and new duds were like armor that would protect her from barbed words and scrutinizing looks. She pursed her lips and blew herself a kiss in the mirror, raising up her hand to grab the rebound of her kiss off of the glass and she chuckled, the sound high and pleasant. Her ears were met with the warbling cuckoos of the clock, signaling it was 10:00 AM.

Beauty sure took a long time, hours that could have been spent reading or watching TV instead.

Showtime!

She snapped up a black knapsack from the kitchen table, careful with its precious cargo, and climbed into her car. Driving with flats felt like driving barefoot. She was too aware of her feet, each small little movement she made when tapping the brakes oddly intimate. Her radio was set to an oldies station playing music that was popular when she was in high school.

Better start checking into good nursing homes that will change your diapers daily, grandma.

A song by Blondie. A pleasing guitar riff followed by the clash and clang of drums and cymbals, and a steely hard voice filled the car, singing, "One way, or another, I'm gonna find ya, I'm gonna get ya, get ya, get ya, get ya!"

She ratcheted up the volume dial as high as it went and sang along in an altogether pleasant voice, staying in tune with the singer. She grinned.

I really am gonna get 'em.

The song ended right as she pulled up to Pastasciutta.

Poetry in motion, the soundtrack to my new fantastical life.

The lights were dark, and a sign propped on the front door just under the name, Pastasciutta, read, *Chiuso*. Although she didn't speak Italian, she knew the restaurant was closed, having already scouted out the comings and goings of the employees in the last few days. The staff didn't usually arrive until an hour before it opened for lunch.

Knowing the front door would be locked, she clutched her black bag and made her way to the adjacent alley. Silver trash cans lined the alleyway and a scraggly black cat glanced at her from its perch atop of one of the can lids. Brilliant yellow eyes bored into her own before turning its focus towards washing its paws with a languid, unconcerned grace. She reached out to pet the cat and then drew her hand back; the last thing she needed was to be mauled by a feral stray. It might put a crimp in her plans if she had to visit the ER with her skin in tatters for a rabies shot and a strong course of antibiotics.

There, an unmarked red door set in the brick wall. She tried the handle, anticipating it would be locked, and was pleasantly surprised when it clicked open. She cocked her head, half-expecting to hear the warbling of an alarm cutting through the silence and was greeted by blessed tranquility.

Good 'ol chef must have forgotten to lock up after himself! Shame.

Luck smiled upon her; she'd brought tools with her just in case she needed to break in, but it looked like fate was throwing her a bone.

Finally.

Her footfalls echoed on the sparkling tile floor, marking her every movement. A faint ammonia smell of cleaning solution wafted up. The kitchen had been buffed and shined within an inch of its life. She could make out her reflection on all the metallic surfaces, not an errant knife or crumb to be found. This place certainly earned its 'A' rating from the health department. An operating room probably wasn't as spotless.

A scent of dish soap hung in the air, along with a lingering aroma of tomato sauce baked into the very foundation of the restaurant. The tangy sauce smell made her stomach whine in hunger.

Should have eaten breakfast, I guess.

However, her stomach would beg for sustenance even if she'd just eaten a *Grand Slam* from Denny's. The atmosphere of the restaurant—even back in the kitchen—served to make one ravenous.

A large walk-in freezer sat in the corner of the room, but recalling Mauricio's horror when asking if any of their catered food was frozen, she didn't bother unlatching the door for a look inside. Part of her was curious what was stored in there since the word "frozen" seemed like a swear word to the sexy waiter, but she didn't plan on finding out.

She spied a trio of fridges across from the freezer.

Bingo.

She opened each door and a *whoosh* of air erupted as the seal between the door and the fridge broke. An army of covered pans greeted her. Their tops had notations in black marker, the writing a masterful cursive—the real cursive she learned in grade school with the weird looking q's and g's. Looping, beautiful, near calligraphy writing designated the pans as penne, chicken and eggplant parmesan, plus a variety of other dishes, with Italian names she didn't recognize. Two of the fridge exteriors were marked with paper reading, *AHS Reunion*. The other fridge contained a daunting number of red tomatoes that were destined to give their lives in the pursuit of authentic sauces.

Three rows of pans sat at the very bottom of the second fridge, all marked with "Tiramisu".

"Better than sex, from what I hear!" Sue whispered as she reached into her bag. She strapped an N-95 to her face, wincing as the rubber strap pulled the hair near her ears; donned a clear set of safety glasses; and snapped on a pair of blue nitrile gloves; all purchased at her local hardware store. She'd nattered on to the bored check-out lady about staining a set of drawers with the proper safety equipment.

Building a good background story in case questions came up later.

Appropriately attired, she pulled out a large metallic cup containing what she thought of as "nut dust". She removed the airtight lid and replaced it with a sieve, purchased at a kitchen goods store explicitly for "dusting coffee onto tiramisu". Again, she'd woven a story in which she planned on tackling her grandmother's tiramisu recipe and had asked the delighted apple-cheeked saleswoman for tips. The saleswoman had assured her she was buying the best product and even threw in an additional sieve "on the house"! People just loved feeling important, and Sue made sure to hang on every word the woman said, acting flabbergasted and enraptured by her recommendation to use mascarpone in the recipe.

No shit.

Sue worked over each pan of tiramisu, tapping the can rhythmically with the heel of her hand, dusting the dessert with a fine layer of the nutty powder. The top of the tiramisu appeared a little lighter than it had previously, but nothing too noticeable. Her metallic can spent, all the toxic dust now made itself a home on top of the delicious appearing Italian dessert.

She glimpsed herself in the buffed metal of the table and chuckled.

I look like a mad lab student!

A clanking noise echoed from the rear, just past the kitchen, intruding rudely on her cheerful thoughts. She jumped back and the metallic can toppled from her hand onto the floor. The sieve broke off of the top with a *clang* that sounded earth shatteringly loud and rolled underneath a gleaming sink. The body of the can jittered to a rest under a neighboring table, its handle just visible.

Her body tensed and she became stock still, ears straining to locate the source of the sound. Each muscle was painfully contracted, coiled, and awaiting orders from her brain; was it gonna be fight or flight?

She should bend and retrieve the can, the evidence of her intrusion, but her body was so taut, tight to the point of burning pain, that she abandoned the idea. Bending over would likely result in her spilling to the floor.

The rumbling of a toilet flushing rang out into the quiet kitchen, followed by several more flushes in quick succession, as if the toilet was choking on a particularly heavy load. The cascading water faded out and she could only hear the faint *whoosh* of water from a sink. Her muscles relaxed some at the sound of cheerful whistling. The interloper hadn't heard the racket she'd made.

But that whistling—initially far away but to her horror, grew louder by the moment.

Part of her felt like giggling at the humor of it all. She'd probably be whistling if she'd had a three flusher shit too, but the survivalist part of her was screaming, *hide, hide*! Her gaze darted about, looking for a hiding place large enough to accommodate her, but everything was so efficiently placed and stored within the kitchen.

Damn, damn, double damn!

Her gaze stopped at the walk-in freezer.

She considered it.

The whistling grew louder, and the notes were punctuated with lyrics—she could make out the tune, "Toxic" by Britney Spears. The lyrics sounded absurd coming out of a man's mouth, especially one accented with heavy Italian inflections. She clamped a hand over her mouth, stifling a case of the giggles threatening to erupt. The prospect of getting caught hadn't impacted her sense of humor, it seemed. In fact, it made everything that much more amusing.

It was always that way, wasn't it? Forbidden

laughter was the most delicious sort.

Moving soundlessly, taking special care to make her steps light, she crossed the kitchen to the freezer and grabbed the latch, which disengaged with a *hisssss*. A faint mist leaked out of the door, snaking out tendrils that dissipated in the warmth of the room. She threw a look over her shoulder as she walked into the freezer, her skin breaking out into goosebumps at the biting cold. It figured, the one day she was dressed like a tart. Normally she would be clad in her jeans and a sweatshirt, which offered much more in the way of protection.

Seeing no one behind her in the kitchen, she pulled the freezer door shut. The lip of the door engaged with a *thump* and she was plunged into stark blackness.

She cocked her head to the side, ears on high alert for any movement in the kitchen, but only heard the faint hum of the freezer's cycling motor.

The cold wicked away the sweat that had broken out in her armpits, causing her to shiver. Her teeth threatened to clang together, and she clenched her jaw to stop them from giving her away—not that anyone would probably hear it, but best not to take chances.

Each breath scorched the lining of her lungs. Intense cold had a way of feeling like searing heat and she was sure that each exhalation would be visible if she weren't wearing the N-95. As visible as a dragon's fiery breath. The mask offered her some protection against the cold, but even with its seal, the frigid air entered like an unwelcome stranger pushing their way inside.

Her nerves from being ambushed by the kitchen visitor had just started to settle when another thought occurred to her.

What if I can't let myself back out?

Alarm bells rang out in her brain and, in her

mind's eye, she saw her hands roaming over the entire inside of the freezer, desperately searching for a release that would return her back to the kitchen.

Could she freeze to death in here?

Already her fingers were numb and stiff, and it wasn't a stretch to imagine them changing first a ruddy red and then black as frostbite set in. The nitrile gloves offered nothing in the way of protection from the cold. She clenched and unclenched her fists, trying to infuse some warmth into them. It's a *freezer* for fuck's sake, it would freeze her just like any of the food stuffs inside it. She thought of a block of frozen hamburger meat and all too easily pictured the muscles of her thighs hardening in the casing of her skin.

Fuck.

The other thing…this was a fixed space with no communication to the outside, right?

What about the oxygen supply?

When this thought occurred to her, she became conscious of her gulping, panicked breaths.

She was gobbling through all her available oxygen!

The N-95 she donned in the kitchen dug into her tender skin, lending to her feelings of claustrophobia. She swiped at it, pushing it down onto her chin. A cascade of cold air beat her mouth like a sucker punch. The elastic straps pinched at her ears, stinging, but the sensation was far away as she took in gulping breaths.

Eating away her oxygen like Pac Man gobbling up multi-colored ghosts .

Fuck.

She forced her breathing to slow down and started taking small sips of air instead of gorging herself in her fright.

I'll probably die from all the carbon dioxide

build up first, instead of freezing to death.

Although the thought of asphyxiating was less than appealing.

At least when someone froze, they just got sleepier as their body shut down and it was said they actually ran hot towards the end—it was why many hypothermia victims were found stripped down to their skivvies.

They called it paradoxical undressing.

She would prefer if some poor busboy didn't find her cold, dead body either completely naked or with her hands around her neck and black tongue poked out from her lips like a bloated leech.

Her breaths came fast again. Thinking of dying had a way of getting her nerves up. The cold air rendered her throat raw as each breath came in grating.

Fuck!

She forced herself to resume the slow rate of

breathing, mindful that each inhalation felt less meaty somehow. The oxygen molecules were ever diminishing, and she desperately needed to get her shit together.

If there was no latch to let herself out, she could just scream until her unseen friend let her out. So, what if she got a charge for breaking and entering? It's not like they were gonna check all the food with a spectrometer to make sure it wasn't tampered with; at most, it would receive a cursory glance to ensure she didn't take a shit in the penne.

Wait a second—her cellphone!

Sure, she could call for help with it, but instead, she thought of its flashlight function.

Light to help her find a way out!

With fumbling fingers, their tips wooden and stupid, she reached into her pocket for her cellphone and clenched her hand around it. She nearly dropped the fucking thing pulling it out, and wouldn't that have been a real bitch? It would surely shatter into pieces and there was no way she would be able to fix it in the dark with deadening fingers.

The phone still radiated heat from her body, and she savored the warmth for a moment before clicking the home button. The screen flared brightly into being, littered with app icons. The cold hadn't seemed to affect the phone yet. The screen was keenly responsive to her movements—even if she couldn't feel them herself. Her index finger shook, but she clicked on the flashlight icon. White light burst into being, illuminating the floor and her feet in a swath of brightness.

Careful to grip the phone in both hands—not trusting her shaking hand alone—she turned her entire body to the left and saw only a blank gray wall.

No latch.

Shit.

She forced her elbows into her sides, attempting to keep rapidly dissipating heat from escaping her core. Her stupid body was trying like hell to achieve equilibrium with her frigid surroundings, even if it killed her in the process.

Fuck the second law of thermodynamics, anyway.

The shivering improved but still, the light jittered in her hands, giving the darkness an eerie feel. Like the shuttering lights of a horror flick, right before the murderer jumps out of a shadowy corner, brandishing a machete behind the virgin heroine.

The virgin always survives 'til the end anyway, so I should be just fine.

Even though her jaw was clenched tight, her teeth continued chattering, snapping together rhythmically like a wind-up toy twisted as far as it could go, then let loose. She thought of a wind-up monkey, clanging its cymbals maniacally, gnashing even rows of teeth shut with each clash.

She turned her whole body to the right, the light jigging ahead of her, revealing ice crusted gray wall and—

—a pair of black eyes.

The unexpected gaze made her jump backwards and her shoulder struck the cold wall behind, sending an electric throb down her arm that instantly rendered it dead and wooden feeling, just like her fingers. A helluva stinger.

Her heart took flight, thumping up against her ribs, each beat a painful tap, and she could hear the pulsing *whoosh* of blood thundering in her ears. She was fearfully close to a swoon, gray dots dancing on the edges of her vision, threatening to coalesce and blot out her sight completely.

Swoon—she'd always thought that term ridiculous, only used in Victorian novels where stupid, weak women *swooned* over a piece of unexpected news, like some eligible bachelor proposing marriage, and had to be revived with smelling salts. But here she was—*swooning*, no scratch that—

This here was *panic*.

This was *fear*.

Had her constitution been weaker or had she been forty years older, the cascading stress hormones might have triggered a lethal arrhythmia that ended it all.

And wouldn't that be a laugh?

Some overworked sous chef would have opened the freezer only to be greeted with her frozen corpse, a rictus grin plastered onto her face.

The face of someone who died with their mental faculties fractured beyond repair. An undertaker couldn't fix that. No, it would have to be a closed casket funeral.

Miraculously, she kept her grip on her phone,

probably because her fingers had more or less frozen into place, and with a trembling hand, summoning up all the courage in her, she cast the light back toward that baleful gaze.

Black eyes meet her own—dead eyes—no consciousness or life force lurking behind them. Even a twinkle from the flashlight of her phone wasn't enough to infuse them with life. Dark orbs floated before her and then she saw they were set in a waxy pale face sporting floppy ears and a snout.

A pig.

Jesus.

A pig carcass hanging in the freezer, set for a meeting with a butcher knife. Diced and sliced into thick, fatty slabs of bacon and nice juicy loins, waiting patiently for its destiny inside some patron's stomach.

Her lovely sense of humor reared its head again.

Poor Wilbur...he certainly went to market.

A metallic creak filled the freezer, the sound horrendous, like nails being raked deliberately along a chalkboard. Her gaze flicked upwards, taking in the chain that Wilbur dangled from. Slowly, his body swayed from side to side, his blank eyes still meeting her own.

Won't you dance with me, Sue?

The leisurely turn of his body and the wretched screech from the unoiled chain made her shiver—not wholly from the cold. Thoughts of graveyards with cracked tombstones partially hidden by swirling green tinged fog entered her head and the spectral clank of chains coming ever closer made her feel like screaming.

And why not? Why shouldn't she take a deep breath and let out a horrendous wail?

No. No. Get ahold of yourself. Breathe.

Martialing all her strength and willpower, she

put her body through its paces, forcing the deep inhale through her nose—her snot there freezing instantly—and a shaky, long exhale.

Better.

She thrusted a hand out, stopping the maddening slow undulating body and mercifully, the horrid noise of the chain ceased at once. The silence should have been bliss, but now more than ever, the freezer was like a tomb—or a mausoleum. And every good mausoleum needed a body—just not hers.

Not today.

A flash of silver caught her eye, just a quick peek behind the carcass sharing the space with her. A reflection of her flashlight or something else? It would be simple to push Mr. Piggy aside to catch a glimpse, but the sheer thought of the clanking metal and the slow dancing pig might actually make her scream. And keep screaming until some nice nurse plunged a needle full of "quiet" medicine into her thigh.

No thanks.

She squinted her eyes shut and forced herself into a hug with the upside-down pig popsicle, her arms encircling its body.

My first dance partner.

As if she weren't already cold, the direct contact from its skin made her nipples ache, turning them into sharpened points that feel like they could break and fall off with the slightest touch. Its glacial skin was mostly smooth under her gloves, pocked by hidden little groves that she imagined might be bristly hairs or maybe small crystals of ice. A quarter turn with her macabre partner, like a waltz, and—Bingo!

A latch!

Hidden in a stupid fucking spot, not right next to the door like one would expect. As if it had been added at the very end of the design process when someone at a meeting asked, "Gee, shouldn't there be an escape latch in there in case some *fuckin' idiot* locks themselves in?"

I hope they gave that guy a raise. Maybe even a corner office and a secretary who wears short skirts and blows him during his lunch breaks.

Her ears strained for any crumb of noise beyond the freezer's confines, listening for a sneeze or footsteps that signaled the kitchen was no longer empty. Only that same maddening silence greeted her, the same silence she was sure resided inside a freshly buried coffin.

A dreamlike quality washed over her, making her feel sleepy and—warm?

Shit.

No time to waste while her body succumbed to hypothermia.

Initially, the handle didn't budge. What if it

was broken or, God forbid—locked?

A small, tinny voice in the back of her mind whispered, *don't worry. Maybe you should just lay down on the floor, curl up in a little ball, get warm? It'll sort itself out.*

Part of her wanted to take the voice's advice. It would be oh-so-easy.

Her hands fell away from the handle, but another voice, a pissed off, bossy voice said, *fuck off! You want all your old classmates to hear about how you died in a freezer? You want to let them turn you into even more of a joke than you already were? They would laugh with glee and ask if there were any Sue-sicles? No! Get moving!*

The thought of their jeering laughter infused her arms with a newfound strength, and, on the second try, the handle budged.

A wedge of light! Blessed fluorescent light from overhead yellow bulbs bathed her face in their glow.

Her body nearly pitched out into the kitchen, but she stopped the impending fall by grabbing onto a metallic table that soon would be littered with cutting boards and sharpened knives.

Maybe even her friend Wilbur! RIP.

Lady Luck was with her; the kitchen was deserted. Kitchen, party of one—her.

She fought a temptation to slide down to the floor into a pile, waiting for warmth to kiss her abused skin. What she wouldn't give for a cup of hot cocoa with swirling marshmallows in front of a roaring fireplace, but it was time to get the fuck out of Dodge.

Put an egg in her shoe and beat it. Make like a tree and leaf.

She let herself back out the side door into the alley and stripped the goggles and N-95 off. She removed the gloves with a snap, happy to see her fingers hadn't turned black or blistered, although the ends appeared a ruddy red.

Maybe frostbite wasn't on the menu!

Careful not to lay bare skin on the goggles or the mask, she shoved her PPE deep into one of the trashcans under the stripped carcasses of some formerly cute little pigs. Friends of Wilbur, perhaps? Flies that looked like engorged raisins with wings sluggishly flitted about and landed on the meager meat, looking for prime real estate for their eggs.

Time enough for a quick brunch before making her debut at the reunion. She smiled; her teeth a dazzling white against her blood red lipstick. The red color masked the underlying blueness of her lips, a nice souvenir from the freezer. Sue peered into her rearview mirror, struck by her beauty in that very moment.

She didn't look like herself.

Two pink blossoms had sprouted up on her cheeks, a nice contrast to the pale cold skin and her eyes positively popped, looking bright and lively. But her smile—rarely seen but mesmerizing like a solar eclipse—revealed white teeth, all uniformly straight except for her canines, which had a somewhat pointed appearance. With her auburn locks, pale skin, and deep red lips—one could imagine her stepping right out of an Ann Rice novel, just as beautiful and arresting as Lestat.

It seemed that a little brush with danger and death could certainly improve a girl's looks!

Chapter Seven

Spearmint flooded her taste buds as she popped another stick of gum, folding the green stick with her tongue before chewing. Her mouth filled with welcome saliva. Sitting in her car outside of the banquet hall ratcheted her anxiety up. All the spit evaporated as a result. It was like the damn Sahara in there!

She gritted her teeth in the rearview mirror, checking for errant lipstick. A sense of pleasure swept through her as she took in her blemish free skin. She felt like a stone-cold fox for the first time in her life. No longer was she the carrot-haired weirdo who was relegated to sitting alone.

Not once dropping her gaze from her reflection, she spoke, rehearsing, "Hello, I'm Sue Moore. How nice to see you all again."

Her nerves threatened to make an appearance as jitteriness bloomed in the pit of her stomach and the repetition acted to steel herself. Years of work with a speech therapist paid off, but sometimes, if she got flustered, her tongue hitched and tripped over the simplest of words. Sputtered uselessly on s's, flattening the r's.

That's not who I am, not anymore, she vowed, the words a protective talisman. It worked. A calm washed over her, like the jets from a warm shower.

Ready or not!

She forced herself out of the safe confines of her car, beeping the key fob twice to engage the locks. Streams of people made their way into the building; she recognized most. Many of the boys from her class had aged into paunchy, balding men while the women bore foreheads that didn't register emotions—Botox anyone? She would bet that most of the women were wearing Spanx, probably more than one pair underneath skintight little dresses.

She made her way to the entrance, forcing her shoulders back, fighting the urge to revert to that ever-so-comfortable hunched-hiding-in-plain-sight-posture her body craved. Another woman walked behind her with a *clack, clack* of high heels, and Sue heard a gasp followed by, "My God, Sue! Is that you?"

Sue turned and made eye contact with the woman. At first, she didn't recognize her, the passage of time obscuring the once known, but she recognized those eyes—an ice-cold blue framed by stark black eyelashes. The eyes right now were soft and kind, but Sue remembered a hard glare to them, a narrow glint.

Britney Reid, one of Lauren Georgia's henchman. While Britney wasn't as much of a raging cunt as her leader, she was still pretty wretched. Once she'd dumped a handful of beetles in Sue's hair during biology and laughed herself into a near rupture while Sue hyperventilated in panic, striking herself over and over in the head with her closed fists.

Oh, they had all laughed! The fuckers were in *tears* each time she struck the beetles, their thick black shells breaking under her fists, warm beetle guts painting her hair and hands a garish yellow.

In English class, they had been paired together by their hippy-dippy teacher, despite Britney's pleas for *any other partner, for the love of God*. The bitch had begged in front of the whole class, her voice pitched high and pleading. Sickening.

Their assigned book, *The Hobbit*, had been met with elation on Sue's part and with a disbelieving groan from Britney. Begrudgingly, they worked together, and Britney softened as time went by. She even invited Sue over to her house for the final project—a poster board. Without an admiring audience, Britney had been downright civil and, gasp, nice! Her mother cooked them a wonderful dinner and Sue sat at the table with the rest of the Reid family, like it was completely normal.

Like she was Britney's friend.

Britney's dad even laughed at one of Sue's jokes! After dinner, Britney admitted she had grown to love Tolkien and the two girls gushed over Middle-earth and its colorful cast of characters. Sue foolishly hoped that she might have an ally in Britney, but once the project was completed, Britney transformed right back into the horrid orc she had always been.

"I almost didn't recognize you!" Britney crowed, throwing her arms around Sue and pulling her into—a hug?

What the fuck?

She squeezed Sue tightly, causing one of the vertebrae in her upper back to pop. Sue's arms were pinned to her sides, not that she would have hugged the monster in return. She was more likely to place her head in a starving lion's mouth.

"Hi." Sue said, her voice quiet. She took Britney in, pleased to see that her previously lithe body had been replaced by a paunchiness not even Spanx could hide.

Never got rid of the baby weight, huh?

Her face was coated in make-up, but no amount of coverup could hide the dark circles that had taken up residence under her eyes.

Her bags are already packed for her next

vacation.

Sue's pleasurable thoughts swirled into a mean glee, making the smile she gave the witch almost genuine.

Britney looked around, as if checking for a hidden camera or bugged microphones and finding none, directed her attention to Sue.

"Hey…so…ah…I wanted to apologize to you…for what a bitch I was in high school." The words came slowly, drawn out as if it pained her to say them. "You didn't deserve any of what we said or did to you…we were real fucking jerks and…well, that was messed up."

She squeezed Sue's shoulder and, without waiting for a reply, breezed inside where a cackling voice erupted, *"Oh my gawd!* Is that Britney Reid? Get over here, you bitch!"

That voice—

Had Sue been a dog, her hackles would have

raised, her mouth drawn into a snarl, and low growls issued from her throat. Instead, her scar burned (*great, now I'm Harry Potter*), and a jet of revulsion ran through her body, like she'd been doused with ice cold water.

Lauren.

That voice still sounded so smug and self-assured; the tone arrogant. Queens throughout history had spoken in the same tones, dismissive of their subjects that existed beneath them. Marie Antionette's words of "Let them eat cake!" had to have been said in exactly the same way.

A high-pitched screech emitted from the doorway. Lauren and Britney were firmly engaged in a meeting ritual that *must* be observed, a custom as old as time. This was accomplished by shrieking in tones that vibrated human vocal cords within an inch of their life. Opera singers strived their entire careers to make similar sounds. The same caterwauls could be heard in lunchrooms, grocery stores, and the like—always when two alpha cunts met. The yawps died out and now Lauren's and Britney's voices mingled, both speaking *at* the other, not listening to the words either of them uttered, but rather, waiting for their turn to speak. The yipping voices grew softer, signaling that the two witches departed elsewhere.

Probably to plan their next Cunts Anonymous meeting.

Sue unclenched her jaw with a creak.

Deep breath in... and out...

She entered the door, finding herself in a room brightly adorned with orange and black tablecloths. Similarly colored balloons littered every surface, and a large cut-out of Tom the Tiger stood in the corner, where guests could insert their stupid heads on Tom's athletic body. She saw Britney crossing her eyes in the cut-out's face while Lauren laughed uproariously and snapped a picture with her phone.

Looks like Tom the Tiger jizzed all over everything in here.

A table with a dazzling metallic orange tablecloth sat adjacent to the entrance and, in alphabetical order, neatly lined up, were name tags. Sue located hers and peeled it off its backing, plastering the name tag just above her right breast.

What a wonderful finishing touch to her outfit, the latest style on the Paris runways!

She walked to the open bar and asked for a bottle of water. She dug in her purse, searching for some bills to offer the bartender.

"No charge for the water, ma'am." He waved off the bills she'd unearthed. Still, she handed him a crumpled bill bearing the likeness of Lincoln. The poor guy deserved compensation for dealing with her asshole classmates all night. She doubted like hell that they would mind their manners and tip after a few drinks.

She didn't share her mother's affinity for alcohol, avoiding it at all costs after she took her field trip to the psych ward, but besides that—the cheapskates couldn't have sprung for an open bar?

Pathetic.

She uncapped the water and sipped, taking in the throngs of people congregating. Just like high school, everyone was clustering together in their predetermined groups; preps, jocks, dorks, band geeks, amongst others.

Lauren and Britney held court surrounded by a gaggle of women who all looked to be on at least their second husband and third plastic surgery, all laughing without moving most of the muscles of their faces. In another huddle, former jocks all looked like they were working on their first coronary judging by their ballooning waistlines that strained the limits of their button-down shirts, talking about this or that game winning catch.

Some things never changed.

A few scattered loners stood around; their knuckles white while they clutched their drinks for dear life.

The voices all grew louder, and Sue heard the telltale slurs creeping into the conversations. People were getting sloshed.

It's okay for them to slur and stutter when they're drunk as skunks, but God forbid, I have a speech impediment.

The din was interrupted by a loud whine of a microphone that made several people protest and cover their ears.

"Sorry about that! Welcome everyone! AHS Class of 2001, *woo-hoo!*" Lauren fist pumped and was answered with a resounding, "*Woo-Hoo!*", the loudest voices coming from the group of aging jocks, whose dicks she no doubt sucked off with gusto in high school. Hopefully, she borrowed their football pads to cushion her knees.

"It's been twenty years; imagine that! And here I am, not looking a day over eighteen!" Lauren preened, and the crowd tittered.

Sue rolled her eyes. *You can't polish a turd, Lauren.*

"Everyone looks amazing, to John Jansen over there in the corner, can you believe he owns his very own car dealership?" John lifted his drained beer, his eyes unfocused, but his smile wide. "And our very own Britney Reid, is a stay at home mommy to a crew of four kids but still manages to be one of the top selling reps of Rodan and Fields in our town!" Britney smirked, her chest visibly puffing out with misplaced pride.

A real Mother Teresa that one, solving world hunger, hugging the lepers, curing cancer, hocking overpriced beauty products.

"All the way in the back, do I spy the red hair of Susan Moore? Wow! Even an ugly duckling can grow up, I guess!" Lauren chortled, a nasty sound, and all eyes turned to Sue.

She felt the heat rise into her cheeks and she forced herself to smile and wave broadly, all the while wishing she could melt into the floor or maybe die of a cerebral aneurysm.

Soon.

"First order of business, a fine meal catered by Pastasciutta." Lauren's lips were almost directly on top of the microphone now, making her voice all breathy. "I hear their tiramisu is to die for!"

Chapter Eight

D r. Brown sat at his computer, relishing the nice day. They were few and far between in this place. He sipped his coffee, eyes closing and rolling back in pleasure, savoring the heat of the brew—normally the coffee was either lukewarm or downright cold by the time he got the chance to drink it.

The emergency room had been slow today, *quiet* even. He only thought the words and only for a second, then wiped them quickly from his mind, as if warding off evil spirits. Words had *power*. Saying the q-word out loud was folly—sheer hubris. Say the word "quiet" and in the next five minutes a hoard of ambulances transporting a tour group of hemophiliacs fresh from "the pointy and dangerous objects" exhibit at the local museum showed up.

Unfortunately for Dr. Brown, his day was about to go to hell. Better drink up that coffee because he was gonna need all of that sweet caffeine when shit hit the fan.

Room five housed a drunk sleeping off a hell of a bender. He'd arrived sans pants and wearing a woman's blouse, but otherwise, all the rooms stood empty. The nurses gossiped at the computers out at the nursing station, sounding like chickens clucking in a coop. The current hot topic of conversation revolved around two of their female co-workers who were engaged in a torrid love affair, despite both of them being married to men.

Such salacious gossip!

The ambulance radio rang out, signaling incoming EMS traffic.

The charge nurse answered the call. "This is Mercy Hospital. Go ahead." She held a pen, poised to take the information from the Medic on the other end.

"This is Medic Ten, onboard we're bringing in a thirty-eight-year-old male. We're coming from a high school reunion where there appears to be an outbreak of food poisoning. He's a bit bradycardic. Suffering from vomiting, diarrhea, a little confused, blood sugar normal. We've started an IV and given him a dose of Zofran and 500 mL NS. We'll be there in five and uh...Mercy? Better get beds ready because there are a ton of sick people here. Must have been some bad salad or something."

As Medic Ten's call ended, the radio crackled to life again...and again...and again.

The story was the same for each call.

Medic Ten trundled in a pale, ashen faced man on their stretcher. His brow dotted with sickly sweat; meager strands of hair plastered to his forehead. His eyes remained closed as he retched and emitted a stream of vomit directly down his front. There was a distinct puke smell, but also—a hint of coffee? Working together, the paramedics and nurses transferred him to the hospital cot. A quick sniff test revealed the man had spectacularly shit himself too.

Soiled himself like a baby.

Dr. Brown wrinkled his nose in displeasure at the feces smell and stood as far away from the man as he could while he performed a physical exam. Standing at arm's length, his stethoscope stretched out to the maximum while he listened to the patient's heart and lungs.

He peppered the man with questions, "Do you

have any medical problems?", "What medications do you take?", and, "When did you start feeling ill?" among them. The man, a one John Jansen of car dealership fame, uttered, "sick" before he passed out, his skin color now bordering on oatmeal gray.

"Shit!" Dr. Brown said, pressing his index and middle fingers to the man's neck, as the nurses moved in a flurry around him, plastering John with stickers that revealed his heart rhythm and vital signs. Dr. Brown didn't need to look up at the monitor above John's head to know what it said. The absence of fluttering movement underneath his fingers told the story.

Flatline.

"No pulse! Start CPR and draw up one milligram of Epi!" A nurse jumped up on the cot, starting CPR and the brittle sound of bones snapping met the ears of everyone in the room. Add broken ribs to John Jansen's list of problems.

Dr. Brown inserted an endotracheal tube, suctioning a large amount of vomitus out of a sickly sweet smelling airway. The team was on their third dose of meds when another EMS cot rolled by in the hallway.

One of the medics perched atop the stretcher, administering chest compressions of their own. "Doc! This one coded on the drive! We've given a dose of Epi, glucose was normal! They just brady-ied down and boom, coded."

"What the fuck is going on here?" Dr. Brown exclaimed, his hands in the air, palms up, as more ambulances poured in. Each rig brought in vomiting, pale patients who lost their pulses shortly after arrival.

The day really took a turn for the worse.

Luckily, Dr. Brown had that cup of coffee earlier! He sorely needed it for the work ahead of him.

Chapter Nine

Sue strolled into the library the day after the reunion. The wrinkled Mildred at the front desk greeted her with a hello and in the same breath said, "Did you hear what happened at the AHS reunion? A bunch of the attendees died!"

She said this in a hushed tone, but there was no mistaking the glittering gleefulness in her eyes. Her voice was full of unintentional smugness, the elation felt when one heard of some horrible, disfiguring accident that has ruined lives, while they themselves sit pretty in their charmed, privileged abodes.

Things like *that* don't happen to people like *them*.

"I was there." Sue said, noting the look of utter ecstasy that crossed the woman's features.

A survivor, here in the flesh! What luck!

"They think it's food poisoning, I guess. I brought my own food to eat." She gave an apologetic shrug. "I have a horrid nut allergy, so I don't take any chances with catering. Too many close calls."

The older woman opened her mouth, intent on peppering Sue with questions, but Sue stalked off, making a beeline to the rack containing the local newspapers. She picked up that day's edition of the Appleton Times and didn't even have to thumb through the pages. The news was stamped right on the front, above the fold!

Just Desserts

Tragedy Befalls the AHS 2001 High School Reunion!

By Sonia Torres

A day that was supposed to be full of reminiscing instead turned into one of the most tragic days in our town's history. The AHS reunion, which was organized by Lauren Georgia-Smith, started out well enough with food catered by hip local restaurant, Pastasciutta.

The attendees savored authentic Italian dishes, all made in-house by Pastasciutta's chef, and capped off the meal with tiramisu and cups of coffee.

The DJ invited everyone to the dance floor, spinning records popular in the early 2000s when several people on the dancefloor complained they felt ill. Many stumbled around before erupting in peals of vomit and collapsing before being taken to local hospitals.

It seemed a rash of food poisoning had broken out but local emergency physician, Dr. Brown was contacted for comment. "No food poisoning that I've heard of causes what I saw today." Most of the members of The Class of 2001 passed away, after being worked on by hospital staff to no avail.

We attempted to contact class president, Lauren Georgia-Smith for comment however, it appears she was amongst those who have passed on.

Police are investigating the mysterious circumstances surrounding these deaths. Please call your local law enforcement if you have any information on this tragic event.

Satisfied, Sue closed the paper, a smile stamped across her face. Such a shame, so many of her former classmates dead, lost to tragedy.

Sue had sat at a table alone, eating her banana and honey sandwich brought from home.

One could never be too careful when dealing with a nut allergy, especially around catered food.

She sipped her bottled water and watched as nearly everyone gorged themselves on appetizers and entrees. Heaped piles of parmesan perched atop the dishes, most swimming with red sauce. The animals used bread to mop up all the stray sauce from their plates, most chewing with their mouths gaping open. Table manners were a distant memory.

God, I hope they don't stuff themselves silly and neglect their dessert!

Sue nervously ripped her napkin into pieces, but she needn't have worried. The fatties saved plenty of room for the famous tiramisu. That legendary second dessert stomach came in handy.

The room had been eerily quiet when dessert was served, the kind of quiet that came only after indulging in an exquisite meal, as if speaking would break the spell of wonderful. Sue politely waved away the plate of the dessert that was thrust onto her table by a caterer.

Better to let someone have seconds.

Eyes rolled backwards in rapture while forkfuls of the decadent mascarpone and dipped lady fingers disappeared into eager mouths. Murmurs of delight filled the room. Several women chattered about how that dessert had been "better than sex!" much to the obvious disdain of husbands within earshot. More than a few plates were licked clean.

The table manners of these animals, Jesus.

They wouldn't pass an inspection by Miss Manners, that was for sure.

They sipped on cups of coffee as the DJ set up his equipment. Stomachs full and happy, if not a bit stretched. Promises were exchanged. "Let's have lunch next week at Pastasciutta!"

Only if they took reservations in Hell.

The main lights dimmed and strobe lights flashed into being.

Thank God I'm not an epileptic!

Sue winced at the vibrantly changing lights splashing across the tablecloth and walls. Most everyone crowded onto the dance floor, their ample bodies moving to Usher's "Yeah", dancing to songs that were popular during the peak of their lives. Perhaps they moved a little slower than normal, their stomachs churning furiously, deep in the throes of digestion.

How sad, really, that most of these people regarded high school as their prime. The men stuck reliving their moments on the football team (who never had a winning season), smelling of rancid sweat from their pads, even after a shower. The women thinking of how *they* had fucked the quarterback (never mind that he turned out to be a total loser, found dead at 24 with a heroin needle in the crook of his arm) and wasn't that just the bee's knees?

Sue watched as they all danced together with a critical eye, watching for what she considered *The Main Event*.

The clock ticked by with agonizing slowness, time lately moving with that languid slowness she'd come to expect. Time had a way of doing that, sensing anticipation and laughing in the face of it. A sluggish hour unspooled before the first spot of action.

A few people stopped dancing, grimaces crossing their faces as they rubbed their stomachs. Too much dancing while being stuffed like a Thanksgiving turkey? The first hints of food poisoning? Low murmurs of conjecture popped up here and there. *"That penne did taste a little funny to me, you?"* And, *"Well, I am lactose intolerant, but I just couldn't help myself!"*

Their movements as they left the dance floor were shambling and erratic, causing some of them to spill to the floor. Teases of too many drinks abounded, although those on the ground didn't see the humor in the joke. A roiling stomach threatening to erupt tended to not be humorous in the slightest.

A lucky minority made it to the toilets before

the puke fountains erupted. The unlucky ones huddled on the floor; their knees drawn up to their chest while they unleashed torrents of vomit. Not enough time had passed for the food to have digested, and soon the dance floor was littered with chewed up noodles floating in piles of puke. The air smelled like spoiled tomatoes and that effervescent *eau de vomit*. Not something you would want to dab behind your ears or on the inside of your wrist.

Their sphincters grew lax, causing most of them to squirt molten diarrhea into their carefully selected outfits. A good portion of her classmates noticed a yellow hue creeping into their vision, their last sights before losing consciousness being a colorful array of yellowish halos.

Sue took it all in, relishing the way Lauren's eyes bulged in their sockets as she vomited down her front, staining her light blue dress. One whole penne noodle clung to the front of her dress, looking a bit like a brooch that was purposefully added to complete the ensemble.

Everything in Lauren's vision had melted into yellow formless blobs and she tripped over her shaky feet, landing on her side with a *thunk*. The fall squeezed the air out of her in a wheezing rush, not that the sound was audible over the retching and wet sounds of barf splashing thickly on the floor.

Her heartbeat by then was beating only twenty times a minute and in a rhythm not compatible with continued consciousness. The black curtain went down then in Lauren's brain, never to be risen again. The theater was closed, the windows shuttered, and the lights blacked out for the last time. Her body convulsed as her heart slowed further, then stopped, bloody foam erupting from her mouth. Her tongue firmly clamped between her teeth, and the seizing movement of her body only helped her teeth gnaw through the delicate muscle and tissue of her tongue.

Plink!

The tip of her tongue dropped out of her mouth, cleanly bitten through. Blood oozed from the remaining stump, filling her mouth with blood that rushed directly into her lungs. Lauren's underpants stained brown with a spurt of diarrhea as her bowels let go—as they often do when someone begins the arduous process of dying.

Sue ambled over to Lauren, mindful to pick a path that avoided the vomit and shit that dominated the floor. She was dressed in new flats after all, couldn't be mussing those up. The pink stump of Laurent's tongue looked just like a wad of bloody chewing gum and Sue bent down near it, careful not to touch the poisonous tongue that had vexed her constantly in her youth. She delicately probed Lauren's throat, feeling for a pulse. Even touching the bitch made her skin crawl with revulsion, like touching the skin of a murderous crocodile, ready to snap at the slightest provocation.

She counted to thirty, really drawing the numbers out, careful to call out *Mississippi* in her mind between each number. Her fingers felt nothing, no fluttering heartbeat during the entire countdown, and with each number, a delightful glee grew larger within her chest.

What a shame, gone young and she had her whole life ahead of her!

She recalled her anguish at all of their taunts, allowing the old hurt to bloom inside her, and she felt the first prickles of tears stir in her eyes.

Perfect, showtime!

A sob erupted from her throat, sounding authentically horrified, and she cried out, "Someone call 911! Lauren's dead!" Her tears made the words come out wetly round and bubbly. Each letter pronounced perfectly.

More bodies fell where they stood, many

figures jerking back and forth through piles of their own or a neighbor's shit, some looking like they were making grotesque snow angels in mounds of puke.

The dry-cleaning bill for all the suits and couture dresses would be murder, but luckily, the dead didn't usually drop their clothes off at the drycleaners on the corner.

Those who hadn't partaken in the tiramisu stood by in wide-eyed horror, alternatively trying to help while remaining puke/shit free; a herculean task. The air was punctuated by cries, begging for help that soon deteriorated into breathless gasps, or even worse, the gurgles of those choking to death on their own secretions. It sounded like music to Sue's ears, more beautiful than any symphony penned by Beethoven in his prime.

I am the conductor of this orchestra, I supplied the instruments, and now the music is hitting an orgasmic crescendo, a climax!

Alligator tears streamed down her face, as she crouched, still bent over Lauren's body in a show of anguish, but her lips betrayed her. The corners turned up and her startling white teeth made an appearance, breaking through the ruby red lipstick she'd applied in the restroom before the dessert course. Had anyone been paying attention, they might have been met with a feeling of disquiet at the mirth of that smile. Maybe they might have raised a few questions.

But as it was, the smile died on her lips unseen, just like the majority of the Class of 2001.

Chapter Ten

Pastasciutta Closed

By Sonia Torres

Pastasciutta, one of Appleton's beloved restaurants, closed its doors indefinitely after the tragedy that claimed the lives of one hundred and ninety-nine people at the 2001 AHS Class Reunion. The graduating class originally contained one hundred and fifty.

However, the death toll climbed higher owing to guests. The restaurant was opened last year by Giuseppe Gorga, an Italian immigrant with a dream of "great authentic Italian food". All the food was made by hand in the restaurant and all meats were freshly imported on the day of service. The restaurant quickly gained a reputation for amazing service, delightful food, and was renowned for their desserts; especially their famous tiramisu, which was an old family recipe handed down through generations of Giuseppe's family. Ironically, only those at the reunion who ingested the tiramisu were among those that perished. Those who opted for the cannoli instead, escaped unscathed.

The restaurant was temporarily closed after the incident and investigated both by police and by the health department. No food codes were found to be violated, nor was there any evidence of wrongdoing. Detective Roosevelt offered a comment, "The entirety of the restaurant was immaculate. We scoured the kitchen and found nothing amiss. Everything was right in its place, other than some random silverware here and there and a dusting can under a table." The restaurant was reopened after being cleared by police, but business has sharply fallen, patrons having developed a bad taste in their mouth, causing the owner to close its doors.

Police have sent all the cutlery, dishes, and samples from the ingredients in the kitchen to the state laboratory for further testing after initial toxicology reports reveal that all those who passed at the reunion had "sky high" levels of digoxin in their tissue samples. A local board-certified toxicologist, Dr. Miller, shed some light on this finding. Dr. Miller stated that, "Digoxin is what we consider a cardiac glycoside and is used medically to treat certain heart rhythms as well as heart failure. Unfortunately, it has a very narrow therapeutic index and overdose of this medication can rapidly lead to death, especially without proper treatment. Most commonly, Digoxin is found in pill form, but it is derived from a plant regularly found in nature; foxglove. Numerous plants in nature contain cardiac glycosides including oleander, lily of the valley, and interestingly in Southeast Asia and India, there is a tree that yields seeds called "pong pong" that are routinely ingested in suicide attempts that tend to be very effective."

The Appleton Times will continue to update regarding the case as more information becomes available.

NJ Callegos

NJ Gallegos

NJ Gallegos writes dark thrillers, odd fiction, and horror, with a strong emphasis on medical horror. When she's not writing, she's work as an Emergency Medicine Physician.

She is currently hard at work on her debut novel, *The Broken Heart*, coming out in the fall of 2023.

She has a chapbook out with Alien Buddha Press, *Only You Can Prevent Forest Fires*. In addition, she has short stories in *Gore 2: A Halloween Anthology*, creepy drabbles in *Drabbledark II: An Anthology of Dark Drabbles*, *Medusa Tales*, and *Sirens Call Magazine*, as well as stories in other Alien Buddha Press compilations.

Bibliography

Drabbledark II: An Anthology of Dark Drabbles, Shacklebound Books, 2022

Gore 2: A Halloween Anthology, Poe Boy Publishing, 2022

Medusa Tales Magazine Issue 1, 2022

Only You Can Prevent Forest Fires, Alien Buddha Press, 2022

Sirens Call Publications E-zine Issue 58, 2022

The Alien Buddha Skips the Party: Part 2, Alien Buddha Press, 2022

The Alien Buddha's House of Horrors #5, Alien Buddha Press, 2022

Connect

Website: njgallegos.com

Vocal: vocal.media/authors/nj-gallegos

Twitter: @DrSpooky_ER

Black Hare Press

BLACK HARE PRESS is a small, independent publisher based in Melbourne, Australia. Founded in 2018, our aim has always been to champion emerging authors from all around the globe and offer opportunities for them to participate in speculative fiction and horror short story anthologies.

Connect: linktr.ee/blackharepress

Terri Hamill

Coming Soon from Black Hare Press

Something in My Eye

by Terri Hamill

Terri Hamill

CHAPTER ONE

According to her diploma, her new job, and her student loans, Jacqui Porter was a doctor of ophthalmology. But at present she was the very junior partner, getting all the crap paperwork, staying after hours to complete the necessary but tedious duty. When her cell went off, showing a call from her best friend, Christina Anderson, she was grateful for the break.

"Hey, Chrissie, what's—"

"Jacqui! Something's wrong with my eye—I can't see!"

She sat up straight. "What? What's wrong? Can you see with the other? When did it start? Where are you?"

Chrissie made a sound a little like a sobbing

gulp. "I'm on my way home, but I pulled over. I was driving, and suddenly it looked like…like a huge bug was crawling across my eye, blocking my vision. It's scared me half to death. It doesn't hurt, there's nothing in it, but…"

Jacqui grimaced. "Is it beginning to thin out?"

"I don't know. Maybe?"

"Okay, how fast can you get here?" She glanced out of her office to see if any of the staff were still there and saw Karen at reception.

"You're closed!"

"Just get here, Chrissie. It sounds like you've got a hole in your retina and if so, I need to look at it now. How close are you?"

"I'm not far, most of the way home. I'll be there in maybe ten?"

"If you don't see me, knock. The door will be locked. I'll wait for you."

"Okay."

Jacqui put her phone down and called out, "Karen! Are you leaving soon?"

Karen turned and craned her neck around the pillar attached to the reception desk. "I've got about half an hour more. Why? Do you need me to stay?"

"No, but Chrissie's on her way here with an emergency. Who else is here? Is Dr. Matheson still here?"

"No, she left. You're the last—as usual."

Rolling her eyes, Jacqui said, "Insubordination; five points from Hufflepuff. Chrissie will knock. Can you let her in?"

Grinning, Karen said, "Sure."

Jacqui rubbed her forehead. Karen was right. She usually was the last one in the office. She guessed it was good practice for the day— someday—when she had her own business. But it still grated to be stuck with the worst patients and the nastiest insurance and government paperwork their part-time practice manager couldn't handle.

Jacqui heard the knock as she was finishing up the reports. She came out of her office as Karen was letting Chrissie in. "C'mon back, I need to check your eye."

Her friend looked terrible, her face red and blotchy. She was keeping her right eye closed. "Thank you, this is driving me crazy!"

It didn't take long to figure out the problem. Jacqui could see it with the scope, even without dilating Chrissie's eye. "Yup. Hole in the retina. It's letting blood into the vitreous humor. That's what you're seeing—so chill, it's not a bug."

The arms of the exam chair creaked as Chrissie's hands tightened on it. "Can you fix it?"

"Me? No. You're gonna need laser surgery." At Chrissie's sharply indrawn breath, Jacqui continued, "Calm down, it's outpatient, and I know a guy. Let me see what I can do. I'll call Ben and blackmail him into getting you in tomorrow." She waggled her finger in front of Chrissie's nose. "No work tomorrow. I'll give you an eye-patch. You shouldn't be fighting to keep your eye closed. And no unnecessary driving. You okay to go home?"

Taking a deep breath and letting it out slowly, Chrissie shut both eyes briefly and nodded. "Yeah. I think so. You sure you can get me in?"

Jacqui turned away, hunting in the cabinets for an eye-patch. "I should. He knows me and this is an emergency, anyway. His office is open later than ours."

"Jacks—"

"Shut up, Teeny-tiny. Are you my best friend or not?" Jacqui whirled around, crossed her arms, and glared at Chrissie.

"You're my *only* friend, Stretch, at least according to you," Chrissie replied, her voice wry.

"And that's not my problem, Miss Introvert

America. I'll get you in, don't worry. I'll let you know when first thing tomorrow. You sure you're okay?"

Chrissie nodded, swallowed, and accepted the eye-patch. "I'll be okay. I need to feed Eddie anyway, before he starts gnawing on the furniture." She stood. "Thank you, Jacks."

Jacqui smiled and hugged her.

"I don't know what I would have done without you."

"Ah, just add it to the pile, Teeny. I'll come over tomorrow with Chinese and see how you're doing."

Karen poked her head in and looked at Jacqui pointedly.

Jacqui gave a slight shake of her head. No, this would be a freebie.

"I'll let you out, Chrissie," Karen said. "I'm leaving, anyway. Don't forget to lock the door, Dr.

Porter, if you ever leave."

"Five more from Hufflepuff for sarcasm!" Jacqui yelled as they left. Then she returned to her office. She had some calls to make.